"Dynamic and inspiring …the Law of Attraction in action! 'Chasing Stars in the Sunshine' inspires readers to design their own destiny and to shine dynamically using the '5 P' philosophy! Follow Molly's lead and live the life you have always imagined ... brilliantly!"

-Anne Sourbeer Morris, Ed.D. (c) Mother of two dynamic daughters, Past President of the Pennsylvania School Counselors Association, Managing Member of A. Morris Consulting, LLC, and 2010 NAPW Woman of the Year

"Molly's endless energy and zest for life are contagious. This book will teach you how to live every day to its fullest, and win with a smile on your most challenging of encounters!"

-Judy Minik, CFO & Vice President, Finance, Conn-Selmer, Inc. (A Subsidiary of Steinway Musical Instruments) and fundraiser for Alzheimer research

"Each of us has a responsibility to improve the world for our children. Molly's '5 P's' are tools that can empower us to lead with our gifts and leave everything a little better (and a little more joyful!) than we found it - including our own lives!"

-Carolyn Commita, Mayor of West Chester, Pennsylvania. Mother and advocate for building a healthy future

"Molly's unbounded energy and her enthusiasm for lifting others are evident on each page of this book. One can't help but feel the sunshine!"

-Beth Yvette Strange, internationally certified Image Management Consultant, co-author of Success Simplified, and mother of seven

"Molly shines bright in every move she makes. Her personal aura is contagious and her practical techniques unveil the inner glow of each individual she touches. This genuine spirit and innate wisdom will pave a better path for humanity as a whole. Godspeed Molly Sunshine!"

-Leslie Padilla, Principal, LPPR,
LLC and Chief Networking Officer,
The Marketing Department,
and mother of two

"Molly not only inspires others to activate their '5 P's' to achieving their dreams, she lives it. If you're striving to transform your life and make your dreams a reality, this book is for you. Through sharing her life experience and her knowledge, Molly demonstrates that anything is possible."

-Ashley Blair Cook, Editor and President of
Phlare magazine, and psychotherapist

CHASING STARS

in the Sunshine

WRITTEN BY MOLLY NECE

**CLAIM YOUR STAR CHASER
COMPANION GUIDE AT**
www.mollysunshinetour.com/chasingstars

CLAIM YOUR STAR CHASER
COMPANION GUIDE AT
www.mollysunshinetour.com/chasingstars

Molly Sunshine Tour.com

Positively Alter Your Life!

CHASING STARS IN THE SUNSHINE

ISBN: 978-1-4507-2586-6

INTRODUCTION

This book was written in true Molly Sunshine style. When I co-authored *Do It Rhino Style* with Dave Magrogan in 15 days, I knew that my story needed to be told so that people of all ages across the country, and even around the world, can be inspired to reflect on their lives, break down any barriers, make what seems impossible, possible, and live their dreams.

With over 15 years of professional speaking experience, I began to pull together the lessons learned and meaningful strategies that have equipped me and others to live their dreams. What started out as a desire to help people find happiness in life, quickly evolved into the simplest, fastest and most effective book on how to realign principles and passions and discover the people and persistence needed to find peace and live your legacy to the Nth degree.

This book was developed from years of proven success strategies that I use everyday in real-life with the people I coach, workshops I lead, keynotes I deliver, and businesses I operate. That's why some call me "Molly Sunshine." You really can enjoy the journey towards achieving your goals and make what others think impossible, possible.

The Molly Sunshine brand is a prime example of making the impossible possible. What started out as a nickname I was given eight years ago, transformed into a book that inspires people to mindfully live their dreams, and has since manifested into a full-blown Molly Sunshine revolution. I've been given the privilege to inspire people of all ages, from Pre-K to Baby Boomers, with the Miss Molly Sunshine children's book series, this book, the Molly Sunshine Tour, and group enter*TRAIN*ment for schools, religious groups, and organizations!

This book is the catalyst for change and greatness. I believe in its message so much that I made available a Star Chaser companion guide. Go to *www.mollysunshinetour.com/chasingstars* to claim your free copy. Share your plan with others. Be empowered to plan and take action so that you can live your legacy to the Nth degree. Here's to making a difference, and being the difference!

Shine on!

Molly

TABLE OF CONTENTS

TABLE OF CONTENTS

No. 1
PRINCIPLES

In Spite of or Because of

Society has been debating the whole "nature versus nurture" argument for years. I have come to believe it is a little of both. A friend of mine once said to me, "We are who we are either because of, or in-spite of our parents." That statement gave me the freedom to choose which attributes I would like to keep, suppress, eliminate, or bring out only when I feel it will help me and others in their life's journey.

To give you a little background, my father is the oldest of eleven and lived on a farm. They didn't have much, but they had love, and one another. My mother is an only child and lived in a small town. Both of my parents have great qualities, but through my lens, they also have their share of challenges. For example, my father has great survival skills. He never received a college education, nor wanted it, and school did not come easily to him. To this day, he still has no idea why he was placed in accelerated courses. His passion was taking things apart and seeing how they worked, not studying.

My mother, on the other hand, received her master's degree in elementary education and taught school until she had my sister and me. Although she felt her education was intended to raise two smart girls, when I left for college I began to see the emptiness. I was uncertain how my parents would get along now that both my sister and I had left home. My mother was a great provider in the home. She cooked great meals, was home for us after school, was strong in writing and foreign languages, kept the household finances, worked part-time for my father, and lived for her children's happiness.

Although my mother liked to stay home and was never a risk taker, my father took calculated risks and lived for adventure and family. My father owned and operated a baby shoe manufacturing company in a small town in Pennsylvania. He blossomed into quite the entrepreneur. He never allowed not having a four year college degree stop him from living his dreams. Being the oldest of eleven, serving as an officer in the military, and growing up a part of a farm family certainly helped prepare him to lead and grow businesses.

Just recently my grandfather died after a five year struggle with Alzheimer's. I've never been to a funeral where I smiled and filled up with so much joy and pride. My father told stories of how they would heat up their water in a galvanized tub with their wood stove and take turns taking their weekly bath. If the water would get cold they would add a bucket of warm water off the stove. In addition, all of the kids would be helping out in the fields at age five and driving a tractor by age twelve. These opportunities as a child shaped what he would later became—a present father, husband, and community leader.

Over the years, he reinvented himself many times over, focused on developing skills and building his networks, listening to leadership audio CDs, surrounding himself with people who knew more than he did, and giving back to his community every chance he had. My dad was never a good reader and would often switch his letters; however, when it came to math and physics, he was a wizard! As a result of all his efforts, he is now in the land development business, serves on multiple boards, and is a leader in his community and church.

Besides being a teacher, my mother has never explored much outside the four walls of the house and the idea of a job scares her. My father often blames himself for her choices in life. In his eyes, he made life too comfortable for her. He finds himself sometimes saying things that I'm sure he wishes he could take back, and my mother wishes he would find someone to go on trips with because she's happy staying at home on their property where she finds peace and solitude. The good news is that when they could have given up and went their separate ways, they decided to see how they could adapt their way of thinking and communicating while still doing the things they enjoy the most.

Why am I telling you this? We are all products of our environment. It's those who don't take the time to reflect and choose what is important to them who are often lost in this big, scary world. Do you see the world as a big, scary, evil place, or a place full of adventure just waiting to be explored? When my sister and I went off to college, we began to see two people living in two different worlds. There was a time when I was afraid that I would have a relationship like my parents. On the flip side, I have since learned to be grateful for their success. They are able to live separate lives, but still persevere and make their marriage work despite their differences. I also have chosen to look at my father's success by giving partial credit to my mother for giving up her career in teaching and recognize the skills she brought to his business.

Self reflection is an integral part to learning, growing, and becoming the person you love unconditionally. It is your choice to focus on the positive attributes you have been given and face the attributes that you know you need to change. In addition, there will always be attributes in others that might not be desirable in your eyes; however, it is your job to look deep inside to find the characteristics that are. You will find as a part of the reflection process that your relationships will grow stronger. I encourage you to take the time to reflect on who and what you have gained either in spite of or because of.

The top 10 lessons I learned in spite of or because of my parents are:

1. Marriage is hard work. There will always be ups and downs, but it's the love and determination to make it work that will help it survive.

2. People change over time. It's a choice to grow together or apart.

3. Because of my father's entrepreneurial spirit and my mother's desire to teach, I am able to run multiple businesses, share knowledge and empower people of all ages, and help others do the same.

4. I have the ability to live my dreams. It's up to me to make it happen! It starts with a goal, a plan, and a lot of action, drive and perseverance.

5. Hurtful words and actions can never be taken back. Showing love and gratitude goes a long way.

6. Differences of opinion doesn't mean there is always a right or a wrong.

7. I've been able to determine how I can help my husband live his dreams, while I live mine, so we both can find happiness together.

8. Make the time to go on adventures together and often. Life doesn't stop after kids. It is only the beginning of a new adventure.

9. It is important to get comfortable about being uncomfortable. Embrace change!

10. I have the ability to control what skills I develop and acquire, and which debilitating attributes I need to address. Blaming others or placing judgment does not help me model the way for others.

Although I chose to focus on my parents, I encourage you to focus on those who played an integral part of your development—for better or worse. List all the qualities that you have gained from them; learn and grow in spite of or because of them.

Virtues According to Ben Franklin

You probably know Ben Franklin as one of the founding fathers of the United States. He was a great leader and diplomat. He signed major documents such as the Declaration of Independence and the Constitution. Maybe you know him as an inventor, or as a scientist who flew kites in lightening storms, or as a writer and printing press operator.

But did you know that in 1726, at the age of 20, while on an 80-day ocean voyage from London back to Philadelphia,

CHAPTER ONE: PRINCIPLES

Benjamin Franklin developed a "plan" for regulating his future behaviors? He was partially motivated by Philippians 4:8: "Finally, brothers, whatever is true, whatever is noble, whatever is right, whatever is pure, whatever is lovely, whatever is admirable—if anything is excellent or praiseworthy—think about such things." He followed the plan that he created faithfully, even to the age of 79 when he wrote about it. He was even more determined to stick with it for his remaining days because of the happiness he had enjoyed so far by following that plan.

The plan he developed was a 13 virtue commitment to giving strict attention to one virtue each week. So, after 13 weeks he had moved through all 13. After 13 weeks, he would start the process over again. So, in one year he would complete the course a total of four times. He tracked his progress by using a little book of 13 charts. At the top of each chart was one of the virtues. The charts had a column for each day of the week and thirteen rows marked with the first letter of each of the 13 virtues. Every evening he would review the day and put a check mark next to each virtue for each fault committed with respect to that virtue for that day.

Naturally, his goal was to live his days and weeks without having to put any marks on his chart. Initially, he found himself putting more marks on these pages than he ever imagined; but in time, he enjoyed seeing them diminish. After awhile, he went through the series only once per year and then only once in several years until finally omitting them entirely. But he always carried the little book with him as a reminder.

Benjamin Franklin's 13 virtues are unique, and obviously

served him well since he is one of the most respected and accomplished men in the history of the United States.

Here is a list of Ben Franklin's 13 Virtues:

1. **Temperance:** *Eat not to dullness and drink not to elevation.*

2. **Silence:** *Speak not but what may benefit others or yourself. Avoid trifling conversation.*

3. **Order:** *Let all your things have their places. Let each part of your business have its time.*

4. **Resolution:** *Resolve to perform what you ought. Perform without fail what you resolve.*

5. **Frugality:** *Make no expense but to do good to others or yourself: i.e. Waste nothing.*

6. **Industry:** *Lose no time. Be always employed in some thing useful. Cut off all unnecessary actions.*

7. **Sincerity:** *Use no hurtful deceit. Think innocently and justly; and, if you speak, speak accordingly.*

8. **Justice:** *Wrong none, by doing injuries or omitting the benefits that are your duty.*

9. **Moderation:** *Avoid extremes. Forebear resenting injuries so much as you think they deserve.*

10. **Cleanliness:** *Tolerate no uncleanness in body, clothes or habitation.*

11. **Chastity:** *Rarely use venery but for health or offspring; Never to dullness, weakness, or the injury of your own or another's peace or reputation.*

12. **Tranquility:** *Be not disturbed at trifles, or at accidents common or unavoidable.*

13. **Humility:** *Imitate Jesus and Socrates.*

Franklin also emphasized these virtues in his *Poor Richard's Almanac*. Although he tried to follow the virtues himself, he sometimes strayed from his good intentions. For example, in his almanac, Poor Richard (Franklin) gave this advice:

"Be temperate in wine, in eating, girls, and cloth, or the Gout will seize you and plague you both."

Franklin relished his food, womanized and sometimes dressed to impress people. His food and wine-drinking habits led him to be plagued with the gout for much of his life. Still, the positive intentions were there. Later, in a letter to his son William, Franklin listed the virtues and recommended that William follow them too. Perhaps you too want to come up with your own list of family virtues to work towards. Make it a part of a family tradition.

I recently listened to a child psychologist speak about how to set up effective family meetings. What a fabulous activity to incorporate your own list of virtues. Measure how well people in the family are living up to the "Family Virtues." Warren Buffet, an investor, industrialist, and philanthropist, recently was asked in an interview "what do you attribute your success to?" His response was he was shown unconditional love and given a solid set of virtues and ethics.

The thirteen virtues are a good guide for you to follow. In fact, keeping track of how well you do in maintaining the virtues and having positive character traits, as Franklin did, is worth trying. You also need to realize that no one is perfect. For example, these thirteen virtues imply that you must be extremely diligent and hardworking. But remember the saying in *Poor Richard's Almanac* that "all work and no play makes John a dull boy," so you can overdo things too. The main idea is to follow the advice of Benjamin Franklin and try to be a person of good character. You will see next, that it goes hand in hand with the importance of seeking your truth.

Seek Your Truth

Reflecting on Ben Franklin's virtues has always inspired me in regards to everyday living. One of my mentors shared with me another fabulous tool—a core principles test. I've adapted it and now use it as a principles guide with many of my coaching clients. It awakens and helps them to understand why they may be in conflict with another person, or perhaps why they are not achieving their goals. Typically, they uncover a misalignment with their value system or the goal in which they are trying to achieve. As a result, it helps them develop a strategy to re-align and adjust their approach so that it is congruent with those principles.

Because of this tool's power to guide health, happiness and productivity, I immediately had the two people I spend the most time with complete it—my supervisor and husband. The results made me shift the way I communicate both with my husband and my supervisor. My husband had 'Self-Respect (pride)' in his top five core principles, so when I said hurtful things like, "Why can't you fix the toilet? Isn't that something that every man knows how to do?" it would trigger him into anger. Looking back it was obviously a poor choice of words on my part; however, it is a good reminder that we are all human and we can all grow from our experiences. We cannot take our words back, however, we can adapt our communication style going forward. Let go of the thought that others must adapt to you. You too play a role in being cognizant of your communication style and where you may need to make shifts.

Another example can be found in my supervisor. He has 'recognition' in his top five core principles. So every chance I get, I verbally recognize him for his achievements. If I used the same approach with his boss, he might think that I was trying to get a raise or needed something in return for my compliment. His boss does not have 'recognition' in his top five core principles.

Seeking truth in your core as well as in others enables you to build the relationships you need to be successful and happy in life. It also helps you to feel confident in your decisions. For example, I have 'health' in my top five core principles. Yet, when I identified them as core principles, I was going to a fast food restaurant at least twice a week and ordering a cheeseburger kids meal with fries and a soda. Did I take out 'health' from my top five principles? No! I did strive to cut out the non-nutritional foods from my diet. Four months later, I was able to do it, and today, I feel great! Something had to change! Of course, it didn't hurt that my husband decided to become a certified nutrition counselor through the Institute of Integrative Nutrition.

Look for accountability partners who have strengths where you have weaknesses. No one is perfect! If you feel you are, you haven't reflected hard enough. My husband is my accountability partner for my core principles of health and family happiness. He brings awareness to me when I am not modeling the way by using a common language we established together. Accountability partners can be a humbling experience at times, but they are the ones who will help you with aligning, sustaining, and strengthening your five P's.

Sometimes a core value is something that we strive for, and some days we are better at achieving it than others. For example, 'family happiness' is in my top core principles, yet I decided to build three companies in three years, raise a family, write four books in six months, work full time at West Chester University, while trying to be a good wife and mother. My health and family began to suffer in this process; two of my core principles were in jeopardy. It was an awful feeling and my business outcomes also began to suffer. Once I realigned my core principles, realigned my commitments to work and family, the success of my businesses multiplied and my family was happier and so was I. It's all a part of the journey. Keep the communication lines open and align your principles with your actions!

Below is the activity I recommend not only for you to take, but everyone around you as well. I encourage you not only share the results with others, especially areas in which you need to improve in order to keep your five P's aligned. Make the commitment to enrich one another and build positive relationships and outcomes.

Take the Core Principles Test

Look at the list of 20 principles below, place a checkmark beside the 15 principles you consider important to you. Of those 15, select ten that are significantly more important to you. Of those ten, circle your top five core principles. It's natural to struggle a little in the process of identifying your top five core principles. These are the principles that will stand the test of time and guide your future success and happiness.

MY CORE PRINCIPLES

- ❑ Family Happiness
- ❑ Power (influence over others)
- ❑ Health
- ❑ Order (stability, conformity)
- ❑ Recognition (status, recognition from others)
- ❑ Integrity (honesty, standing up for oneself)
- ❑ Advancement (leadership positions, sports, classes)
- ❑ Helpfulness (helping others, improving society)
- ❑ Loyalty
- ❑ Creativity (imaginative, innovative)
- ❑ Adventure (new challenges)
- ❑ Wealth (getting rich, making money)
- ❑ Involvement (being involved with others)
- ❑ Wisdom
- ❑ Self Respect (pride)
- ❑ Economic Security
- ❑ Competitiveness (winning, taking risks)
- ❑ Responsibility (accountable for results)

❑ Friendship (close relationships with others)

❑ Inner Harmony (being at peace with oneself)

Live Life by Example

One of my workshops I facilitate is called, "The Legacy Lecture Project." Participants are asked to reflect on their legacy and identify what or who have helped them live their legacy. One group struggled immensely with the question, "Who do I value as a leader and why?" I had to ask the question differently in order to get them to the same outcome. I asked them, "What did you learn not to do from the leaders you've encountered in life?" Another group I asked, "Describe what an exceptional leader would look like?" Through my experiences, I've discovered that people struggle with finding people who have all the attributes they admire.

If all of us took the time to reflect on what a true leader is and live their life accordingly, we would live out Gandhi's challenge to the world. Mahatma Gandhi challenged us to, "Be the change you want to see in the world." People think that there are certain people who are leaders, but yet they forget that each day we have the choice to lead; whether to guide our children, volunteer in our community, or take on an extra project at work. We have limitless opportunities to lead.

Having said this, someone once told me a story about Gandhi. It impacted me and the way I approach life, and it has the power to change the world.

During the 1930's, a young boy had become obsessed with eating sugar. His mother was very upset with this. But no matter how much she scolded him and tried to break his habit, he continued to satisfy his sweet tooth. Totally frustrated, she decided to take her son to see his idol, Mahatma Gandhi. Perhaps her son would listen to him.

She walked miles, for hours under scorching sun to finally reach Gandhi's ashram. There, she shared with Gandhi her predicament. *"Bapu, my son eats too much sugar. It is not good for his health. Would you please advise him to stop eating it?"*

Gandhi listened to the woman carefully, thought for a while and replied, *"Please come back after two weeks. I will talk to your son."*

The woman looked perplexed and wondered why he had not asked the boy to stop eating sugar right away. She took the boy by the hand and went home.

Two weeks later they revisited Gandhi. Gandhi looked directly at the boy and said, *"Boy, you should stop eating sugar. It is not good for your health."*

The boy nodded and promised he would not continue this habit any longer. The boy's mother was puzzled. She turned to Gandhi and asked, *"Gandhi, why didn't you tell Bapu that two weeks ago when I brought him here to see you?"*

Gandhi smiled, *"Mother, two weeks ago I was eating a lot of sugar myself."*

Think about some of your past actions. Would some call you a hypocrite? Do your actions match your words? Think of your actions through the eyes of a five year old. Would he or she approve of the approach you chose to handle a difficult situation? How you have chosen to live your life is the legacy you have chosen to leave—for better or worse. Establish your principles, live by them daily, and set the example for others.

The Struggle for Power

We can all agree that we are categorized as homosapiens. In addition, ego is in our chemical make up. We often experience the "survival of the fittest." We're either struggling or thriving. When we are born, we have the natural instinct to fight to survive. When babies are hungry or in discomfort they will cry and seek food and comfort at all costs. Ask a baby if he cares that his mother only had two hours of sleep. Although he or she couldn't respond, we all know the answer. As we grow, the power struggle turns into war, unhealthy competition, corrupt governments, unethical business practices, an outdated education system, consumer exploitation, and the list goes on. Studies found that, on average, seventy-five percent of a person's day is filled with negative contextual images or situations.

My father asked me why I don't watch the news every night. In return, I asked him, "Why should I?" His response to me was so I can speak intellectually about what is happening in the world. I told him that my focus is on the things that I have control over. Right now I am busy trying to uplift the world, not be deflated by it. Some day perhaps I will be given the opportunity to solve some of the world's "bigger" problems. For now, I choose to help inspire and equip those who can fix the "bigger" problem and help enlighten those who are fueling "the problem." The subject never came up again.

People often look for power outside themselves; perhaps in material things or in other people. What they seem to forget is that they have the raw, natural power inside of themselves to make a difference and not become a part of the problem. There are many people we can help each day. It might be a kind word or a gentle smile. In my 20's, I approached people who thought status quo was acceptable very different than I do today. You might say I was stuck in my own power struggle. I didn't understand how people could be allowed to behave in a way that did not treat the customer with respect, and that there was little to no urgency behind what they were doing. In addition, work was being assigned to those who could get the job done, and as a result, they burned out and moved onto other organizations. The supervisor would respond, "Well, I knew that would happen. It always does." Yet nothing ever changed. These status quo people knew I had no respect for them, and they saw me as a new kid on the block, trying to make them do more work. My energies were being wasted on a population who neither wanted to be held accountable for their actions, nor were their supervisors interested in holding them accountable. I started to become very bitter and resentful, something very inconsistent with my principles.

One day, I woke up and said, "Oh my goodness, people are seeing that I may be part of the problem, not a part of the solution!" That is the day that I refocused my energies and decided to get a Master's Degree in Training and Organizational Development. I discovered how I could rechannel my gifts and energies into something where I could make a positive impact and be a part of the solution. In my experience, I discovered that supervisors needed as much if not more coaching and support than the employees themselves. Unfortunately, supervisors sometimes are the last to say they need help because they see it as a sign of weakness or they don't have time—again, that awful power struggle that can eat up one's soul if it is allowed to happen.

As a result of my newly acquired knowledge, I was fortunate enough to have someone who saw my gifts and began assigning me additional projects not remotely related to my current position. It eventually turned into a new position as a Training and Development Specialist. Having said this, creating a new position in this organization was almost unheard of. It just shows you again that you can make the impossible, possible. After the promotion, some employees told me that I was lucky, and that they wished that they could do something like that. I shared with them one of my favorite quotes by Seneca, "luck is where preparation meets opportunity." Today, I regularly help people discover and live their legacy. As a result, they find themselves in situations where they are rewarded for their hard work and self-discovery.

The bottom line is there always seem to be power struggles going on in practically every environment and at every level of any organization. Don't forget that you have control over your own source of power. Do you want to use your power source for good, or cause more discomfort, pain, or anguish for others? Identify your power struggles and realize that everyone deserves a second chance. After reaching out, my organization knew I had a gift that needed rechanneling. Explore your source of power and rechannel it for the greater good. If you discover that your 'power source' is not welcomed, keep exploring other adventures and adapting along the way. We all should be growing, adapting, and strengthening ourselves along the way. There is a place for everyone in this world.

STAR POWER ACTIONS

1.) List all the strengths you have because of your parents, guardians, and/or mentors. Then, write a hand-written letter thanking them for those qualities you acquired because of them. Be specific! It is never too long of a letter when it comes to sharing gratitude. This is something they will hold onto and cherish for a very long time.

2.) As I have done in this chapter, list all the things you have learned in spite of your parents or guardians. Then, write a hand written note to yourself congratulating yourself on these achievements.

3.) List all the areas where you need to overcome something. We all have something! There is always some area of our life that we want to enhance or improve. We'll come back to these later in the book.

4.) Sit down as a family and come up with a list together of "family virtues." Some may be easier to attain for some members of the family than others. Be sure to celebrate successes along the way. Positive reinforcement is the best way to experience repeated behaviors. Set a time each month when you will talk about what is working well and where the challenges lie.

5.) Have each member of the house take the "principles test." Approach this activity without judgment. See it as an opportunity to enhance communication and understand what matters most to each individual. Celebrate individuality!

6.) Think of a leader that you admire and respect. Write down why and see how you can adapt your life and live by their example.

7.) Search for a short story that gives you strength and re inforces the virtue you are trying to strengthen most.

8.) Identify what causes you to go into "bull in the china shop" mode. What positive strategies will you take that will help you use your power for good, not disruption?

9.) Do you have a "gift" that needs rechanneling? What is it, what are you going to do about it, and when will you know that it has been rechanneled?

"I can honestly say that I was never affected by the question of the success of an undertaking. If I felt it was the right thing to do, I was for it regardless of the possible outcome."

–Golda Meir, Fourth Prime Minister of the State of Israel

No. 2
PASSION

Live Intentionally

The Law of Attraction states that you create what you think about. If you become aware of this law and begin to work with it, then your thoughts become conscious intent. Why then does it seem that we keep getting the "same old, same old" instead of what we want? Hold on readers, I'm going to get scientific for a few moments for the possible skeptics out there.

The problem could lie in the five senses of perception. Through the senses of sight, hearing, touch, taste and smell, we bring in information that is interpreted in a particular part of the brain. The sensory integration center's task is to coordinate the information into a cohesive whole. When there isn't cohesiveness we can "spin out" in disorientation. A simple example is our sight. The brain takes what we see from two eyes and makes it into one vision instead of two.

The integration center uses stored information in other parts of the brain to help it with its interpretations. This creates a "perceiving everything the same" attitude. The hypothalamus, which lies near this center of the brain, stores trauma information. If the sensory integration center only relies on the hypothalamus for information, then we will continue to perceive every response to us as some form of trauma.

To counter the brain's shortcut mechanisms of using stored information to interpret our world, we can use our frontal lobe (the thinking part of our brain) to perceive in new ways. When you have a conscious intent for something in your life such as a new job, new car, or higher income, you then consciously choose to perceive anything that supports that intent.

In quantum physics, this is called Observer-Based Reality. What quantum physicists noticed is that when they observe a quantum particle, it became exactly what the observer expects it to become. Napoleon Hill, author of "Think and Grow Rich," calls it "acting as if;" this means I adopt the attitude that what I want to be is who I am. The Universe is responding to my intention. Why wouldn't it? Then, I look for the signs that my intention is manifesting.

Although some people call this magical thinking, this simple but profound mental attitude energetically realigns, or reprograms your sensory integration center to a reality that includes your intention. When I'm looking for signs I'm never quite sure how or in what form the signs will show up. Maybe somebody around me speaks about my intention, without any prompting on my part, or maybe I find a smaller version of what my intention is about. Whatever the form, I allow myself to be alert for those signs so that it increases the energy around the intention.

When you state an intention, you must believe that the universe will respond. Those who pray know the power of prayer. Why do you think there are prayer groups? It works. So whether you believe in a God or a higher power, it's your intention, your vibrations, your actions, that help you reap what you sew. You see what you are trying to draw closer to you. How the intention becomes manifested is part of the great mystery of living. It depends on your own belief system. No matter what you believe, the two biggest tips I learned early on is to stop trying to figure it out, and that there will always be skeptics working against your beliefs. It is a part of life. It is up to you to decide how you want to approach it.

My parents, sister and husband were all skeptics about how I was able to attract all these amazing people and events into my life, and to an extent, they still are. They have their own journey to travel and set of beliefs and perspectives. As my journey unfolds, they are finding it harder and harder to be skeptics—coincidence is no longer a feasible explanation.

When I initially told them about the book, "The Secret," and philosophy behind the Law of Attraction, my father, being of an engineer's mind, thought I lost my mind. My mother, who seems to attract everything negative into her life, wasn't about to start believing in this "nonsense." My sister said that it was all coincidence and my brother-in-law thought that it was just "Molly being Molly," trying to change the world. The only person who was slightly interested in it was my nephew who was more intrigued by the idea than anything. My husband was quiet early on until one day he just gave in to the philosophy. Everything was way too surreal for it not to be true.

After sharing story after story with my family, they stopped protesting the Law of Attraction concept because my journey has been and continues to be so amazing. To this day, my parents continue to try to chalk it up to my being a "go-getter." I don't deny that it definitely takes actions to achieve goals; however, if I wasn't out actively sharing my intentions with the universe and making the connections, it would be like me playing the lotto expecting to win every time.

Here are some tips to help you attract people and situations into your life based on my experiences:

• **Be conscious about your intentions.** Focus your mind on your heart by tying it to an emotion. From that place ask yourself, "What would I like to see happen?"

• **Always state your intention in the positive.** Many of us are used to focusing only on what we don't want. This can be a helpful stage in identifying what we do want but the body won't heal if it doesn't have a sense of forward movement.

• **State your intention in the first person.** If your intention is, "My partner needs to be more loving," it won't work because of free will and choice issues. Instead, identify that you want to feel loved, cherished, adored, etc. and ask for that. Be specific and anchor your intention to an emotion or feeling word.

• **Be explicit.** Many of us use shortcuts in our communication, implying certain things without actually saying them. The Universe is very literal.

• **Be open to outcome.** Many of us block that which we most want to receive or limit our intentions by expecting them to be in a particular form or timing.

• **Release your intention to the Universe.** After stating it, let it go energetically. The mind is not the "doer" but the "director." Staying too connected to the intention is similar to micromanaging your staff.

• **Keep a journal of your intentions.** Observe what begins to shift and change in your life. As you do, you'll begin to understand how intentions work in the world. At the same time you'll begin to trust the Universe to respond to your intentions.

• **Bring your new awareness to others.** Intentions empower. Invite your children, spouse, partner, coworkers, etc. to state their intentions before starting a new endeavor. When talking with people who are endless complainers, invite them to shift their focus by saying, "What would you have liked to have happened?"

Engaging the Flow

Now, some of you might be thinking I've lost my mind, others are thinking how cool would that be if it was true, while others know exactly what I am talking about. While in my student teaching semester in college, I bought the book, *Song of Celestine*, to read to my class. Just recently, I discovered that there is a book and a movie by a similar title, *The Celestine Prophesy*. I encourage all of you to read or watch it.

In his book, James Redfield shares with us that there are eleven scrolls and that the chaos in this world is changing us. This change is going to cause an awakening that will make us look at the world through a different frame of reference, perspective, or point of view. The seventh insight is "engaging the flow." In other words, we must know our personal mission to further enhance the flow of mysterious coincidences as we are guided toward our destinies. First we have a question; then dreams, daydreams, and intuitions that lead us towards the answers, which usually are synchronistically provided by the wisdom of another human being.

Three years ago, this seventh insight is exactly how my one business evolved into three by my third year in business. All my life I had the passion to help others. I received my degree in elementary education and psychology in 1996 from Gettysburg College and received the student teacher of the year award, yet the classroom wasn't calling me. I felt like I was being called to work with college students. I enjoyed my experience in the world of higher education, even my stint in corporate America, but there was something else I was being drawn to do. While building my skills and my networks, I continued searching—engaging in the flow.

When I took the job as West Chester University's Training Development Specialist and now as their Senior Internal Consultant, I knew I was on the right path. I designed and facilitated many keynotes and workshops for students, faculty and staff. There was something inside of me telling me I had to do something for high school students.

While watching *Caddyshack*, I asked the question, "What can I be doing to link high school students to people in the workforce to better prepare them for the world of work?" The answer quickly came to me. I would create an internship database system that would link high school students, schools, and businesses together so that they can get exposed to businesses, occupations, and skills needed to be successful in the world of work. Working in organizational development, I was familiar with the challenges that lie ahead with baby boomers starting to leave the workforce and taking their knowledge with them.

I had to do something to shorten the learning curve for these students and give them an opportunity to explore careers prior to jumping into them after college graduation, only to realize that this wasn't their calling.

I met a professor at West Chester University who not only had the computer programming knowledge, but the passion for helping students. I also met a woman who told me about a project that a local school district was working on where MyInternshipGopher.com could be welcomed. That same woman led me to another man who knew a woman at an economic development council who might want to support the initiative. That led to a local chamber's interest in partnering. At a chamber luncheon, I met Dave Magrogan, a self made millionaire, which led to my partnering with him to build our Rhino Living Training Group.

A few months ago, a good friend asked me if I recalled what I told him the day I met Dave. He recalled me saying that, "I am going to make something happen today and it is going to involve Dave Magrogan." Never having met Dave, I made sure to sit by him at lunch. Just then, a gentleman I met a few months prior, sat down between us. When he sat down, he commented to me that he "better hold on tight." Not knowing what he meant, I soon found out. There was synergy from the beginning. Dave and I were two passionate people wanting to make a difference in the world.

After hearing him speak, I told him that we need to partner and share his message with the world! Two weeks later, Dave and I formed our training company, Rhino Living. He took a leap of faith. He never met me before, but went with his intuition. One year later, Rhino Living had a following of 6,000 people, a website, blog, weekly inspirational e-mails, workbooks, train the trainer program, DVDs, teleseminars, workshops, keynotes, and a book we wrote in 15 days. Did he put me on his payroll? Nope! It was all built on sweat equity. My father couldn't believe I was doing everything for free, but what I was gaining was worth far more than money.

Because of helping build the Rhino Living brand and my experience in designing and facilitating 40 interactive workshops and keynotes, a third business was born. Through Legacy Producers, I coach and consult people "how to live their legacy to the Nth degree." In other words, I help people create their brand and share their message through books, keynotes, blogs, websites, film and music. I was also inspired by Randy Pausch's Last Lecture at Carnegie Mellon University titled, "Achieving Your Childhood Dreams." You can view his lecture on YouTube. It will change your life and how you choose to view your own legacy. Having said this, I shared my Legacy Producers business model with one of my mentors, and he just happened to know the co-author of The Last Lecture, Jeffery Zaslow, best selling author and columnist for the Wall Street Journal. The lesson learned here is to share your passions with others and live your principles daily.

Surround Yourself with Inspiration

As intention states, you will be given signs to when you are on right path, when you need to adapt, or engage others in the flow. My five year goal is to make a difference in 500,000 peoples' lives by 2015. I have it posted on my mirror in our bedroom so it is the first thing I see in the morning and the last thing I see before I go to bed. I also give credit to being able to build three businesses in three years and write four books in less than a year because of what I surrounded myself with over those years.

Recently I bought a yellow PT cruiser to help me brand and promote the Molly Sunshine Tour. It also keeps me focused on my goals, but also what I have set out to accomplish that day. The yellow PT cruiser is just one of the many things I choose to surround myself with to keep in the flow and keep the positive energies high.

I didn't always know the power of surrounding myself with "things" that will help inspire me to reach my goals. Early in my journey I noticed that things with spiral designs and butterflies surrounded me. I also was drawn to sunflowers and nature. I thought it was bizarre so I decided to Google the hidden meaning behind butterfly. I knew it had to be a sign for something. In ancient Greek the word for butterfly is "Psyche," which when translated means "soul." In addition, metamorphosis is a symbol of change and joy.

When I researched the Celtic spiral symbol, I discover that it meant "evolution and holistic growth, awareness of the one within the context of the whole, and connectivity and union with energies." At this point in my journey, I thought that I must be heading in a positive direction and onto something good. What that "something" was I didn't know; I had to trust the universe and continue to look for signs. Think about the things that make you happy or things that remind you of your passions and dreams. Post them in public places so that you can be reminded of the goodness that is yet to come. It will help you keep your dreams and happiness front of mind and refocus you when you are having a bad day or not modeling your core principles.

While what I just described was all visual and physical signs of intention, don't forget the other senses. Create an inspiring CD that has all your uplifting songs on it, or in my case, create your own song! I met a man who was recommended by a student to teach Tai Chi for employees. I'm up to trying anything once to see if it is something that employees would enjoy in hopes of relieving some of their daily tension and stress. Mitch and I immediately connected. After the class I told him that I knew our paths would cross again, but I wasn't sure how or when quite yet. He had the same feeling, but he couldn't pinpoint it either; however, we both made our intention known. I encourage you to do the same when you meet a person you feel remotely connected to. Don't spend a lot of time trying to figure out why at first, but I encourage you to see how that person is aligned with your principles and make note of their passions.

Mitch came back into my life last summer. I had the thought of making up my own parody such as Anita Renfroe did with her "Mom's Song" to the William Tell Overature. I encourage you to watch it on YouTube. It is hilarious! I always had a thought of writing a parody to *The Saints Go Marching In*. I added it to my vision board— that happens to take up one whole wall of our guest bedroom! What I discovered was that Mitch was also was a Grammy Award Winner music producer and remixer of some pretty famous artists in the late 80's early 90's. I told him that when the lyrics come to me, I would like some time in his studio. He was on board and excited to help me live out my passions!

One fall Sunday morning I decided to revisit the parody project. I even downloaded the track off of iTunes. The family went to church, and when we returned, the "Oh Legacy" lyrics came racing out of my head and onto my computer screen in less than 30 minutes! Not only did I write them, I went into the studio, sang it, designed a mini movie and uploaded it onto my Legacy Producers Channel on YouTube three days later. It's 100% passion! Did I mention I never took a singing lesson in my life? My best friend from elementary school, and still today, she jokes with me because I never sing the exact words to songs. My boss teases me, "You're not going to sing, are you?" It was not uncommon on a challenging day at the office for me to begin singing Gloria Gaynor's song, *I Will Survive*. You need to find the song within yourself to get you through the tough times as well as the good times. Tyler, our five year old, is now making up lyrics to songs—his most famous YouTube song we created together is "You Got to Give to Receive."

If you would like to have fun and sing along with the whole family, here are the lyrics to "Oh Legacy," or better yet, make up your own family "5 P's" theme song!

So legacy… where do you live?
Are you happy where you are?
What is your destination?
How are you gonna live on?

Oh legacy… where have you been?
I've been looking for you still.
What I found while I was searchin'
Is you were right there all the time.

When the stars… came bright as day,
I knew which stars were mine to stay.

I just had to see my dreams
In God's big plans for me.

Some say we have no hope.
I say don't sell yourself short.
Look for people who take you farther
And help you live your legacy.

When judgment day… comes around,
I know that this world will be better.
Just because I chose to give
My legacy to the world.

What Legacy… do you want to live?
Just don't sit and wait for it.
Go discover what you should be doing
To make a difference in this world.

It is important to surround yourself with the things that
"light you up" inside, not drag you down. Find your space
to map out your visions to keep your 5 P's front of mind.
It helps to remind you of your purpose and what is yet
to come. It may change over time and things will be
added and taken down, but you must start somewhere.
A children's book has been on my vision board for
five years. I wrote my children's book, A *Tale of Miss
Molly Sunshine*, while watching an inspiring movie I
picked up at the local library called, *The Blue Butterfly*.
Two days later I saw a blue butterfly from Guyana
preserved naturally in an Amish store window. I brought it
home, and I had it beside me the entire time I wrote this
book. It served as inspiration.

When we were finished recording the book audio for *A Tale of Miss Molly Sunshine*, my son asked me, "Can I have my own book, Mommy?" In a look for signs and an inspiring moment, I replied, "Sure, Sunshine!" That night, after everyone went to bed, I began to think about what made Tyler special. Tyler is a curious child who loves adventure and never hesitates to take a risk. He also loves music. Singing and dancing brings joy to his life--and ours! He loves the water and dreams about being an animal keeper at a zoo and running his own aquarium one day. After two hours into brainstorming, the story came to me like a tidal wave. Another Miss Molly Sunshine children's book was created—*Tyler's Tidal Wave Adventure*.

A few months later, I e-mailed my mother and asked her if she knew where my children's book I wrote and illustrated in high school and presented to the local school board was located. She didn't recall the book, but she looked in a few places in their house where she thought it might be. Although she was not successful, we visited them the next weekend. I felt the intuition to go up to their attic. There were two boxes of my student teaching material. I looked in the first box and the book was the third book from the top. I read the hand bound laminated book, and the storyline had uncanny similarities to *A Tale of Miss Molly Sunshine*. In the "about the author" section it said that Molly will be writing more books and making a difference in the world. It left me speechless since my life's motto is "make a difference and be the difference," and I am now an author. Another incredible story that will help me inspire others of all ages to live their dreams and keep their 5 P's front of mind.

Think about what inspired you as a child and compare it to what inspires you now. Are there any similarities? What did you want to do when you "grew up?" Who did you want to become? Are there passions that have fallen off your vision board that you would like to add? What can you do each day or week that can help you move towards fulfilling those passions?

Inspire Others with Your Presence

About ten years ago, two West Chester University colleagues decided to give me a nickname, "Molly Sunshine," and it stuck. No matter what task I was given, or curve ball I was thrown, I worked through it with a smile, a positive mental attitude, and some type of plan. When I recently told a friend of mine about my children's book, she informed me that in college people always called me the ray of sunshine. Although I didn't recall this, I guess "Molly Sunshine" was always intended to be.

How you portray yourself to the outside world is what you are going to attract into your life—both good and bad. It can be a cruel world out there, but like your principles, you have the choice as to how you are going to portray yourself to others. Some may like you, some may love you, but some may not be able to stand you, and that's OK too. One of my mentors told me that it is best to be who you are so you attract who you want to do business with. At the time I thought he was nuts because I wanted to do business with everyone. I'll tell you right now, no you don't!

What I do recommend is seeking perspective from people you trust and are truth tellers as to how they feel the outside world views your presence. Include people who are close to you (kids included) and acquaintances; include varied personalities and communication styles. Share with them what you are looking to attract so that they can give you meaningful feedback. This is your opportunity to celebrate what you are doing well, and reflect on how you may choose to adapt your presence to attract what you want to experience in your life. Never become defensive with those who give you feedback. Instead, politely ask for examples that back up their perspective. They are entitled to their own opinion. Remember, each person comes with their own frame of reference too. Be open to other people's perspectives. It is a great way to grow, learn and strengthen your relationships.

Here are a few questions that can help others assess your presence and give you action steps to attract what you want out of life:

1. What are the first five attributes that come to mind when you think of me?
2. Without me opening my mouth, what does my appearance say to you?
3. When in conversation, what do you like most about my communication style?
4. What comes to mind when you think of a person with a pleasing, enjoyable presence?
5. In your opinion, what are some helpful strategies that could help me achieve that level of presence?

How you present yourself determines who you are going to attract. If you show up to meetings late, you are going to attract others who show up to meetings late, or worse, miss deadlines and don't give you what you ask for. Those are the people who will take up the most of your time. Remember back in school when you were placed in group work, and you were paired with the one person that no one wanted? Are you exhibiting any of the behaviors of that student that no one wanted on their team? If you are, stop it! How are you going to live your legacy if you can't get to work on time or meet deadlines? When I coach clients, I take them back to these simple must do's of having presence and what that means to them and their clients. I am surprised how much time I spend with some clients on the topic of presence. However, it is the foundation of their future success.

I never saw myself as the good looking one in high school. Quite frankly, people could have called me "zit-face" for what seemed to be a lifetime. I learned early on how to overcompensate for my outside appearances through leadership, collaboration, and hard work. Eventually, I was voted prom queen and given senior superlatives such as, "best smile." I often tell clients who are struggling with their self-esteem that one of my greatest gifts was lacking outside beauty. This is called positive reframing. It's when you take something negative and turn it into something positive. Although it was a tough time in my life, it is all how I chose to react to life's curveballs. I encourage you to catch yourself when you have a negative thought and see how you can positive reframe it. If you are having trouble reframing it, go to the most positive person you know and ask for help! If you don't have a positive person in your life, immediately put it on your vision board and ask yourself what you are going to do to attract more positive people in your life.

I want to make the time in this chapter to define what I mean by outward presence and how it can dictate your future success. I'm not talking about name brand clothes either. I remember when someone who dressed like a million bucks (because it probably did cost her a million bucks) said to me how much she liked my jacket. When she asked me where I bought it, I proudly said Target to see what she would say. It's what I call the "Materialistic Friend Test." Her reaction was, "I can't believe that. It's gorgeous!" I kept her as a friend. Now if she would have wrinkled up her nose and said "oh," I would know that she is definitely someone I don't need in my inner circle. I have discovered that "materialistic" people have a greater chance of being "Negative Nancy" and can take you off your path to reaching your goals.

Another piece of valuable advice I give to all my keynote and workshop participants is to have an answer for "What's up?" It helps you establish your presence. Are you going to talk about the latest TV show you watched, or what your husband did wrong? Or are you going to focus on the positive and share something positive and talk about an exciting project you are working on? When I go out in public, people can't wait to ask me the question, because they know I'll be working on something with my businesses, community or family that is exciting, new and different. This strategy will help you stay focused on the positive.

Don't put the negative energies out into the Universe. It not only will affect your presence, but also could prevent you from achieving your dreams, or finding the people who want to help you reach your goals. For example, everyone who is a part of The Molly Sunshine

Tour shares similar passions, brings their own special gifts to the tour, and are principle driven people with tons of passion and energy. I attracted them to me because of either who I am or what someone who they value told them about me. I also took action and reached out to a few people as well. It's not always about your connections, but also how you approach making that personal connection.

When you are given a chance to meet someone who can impact your life, be sure to have an answer for "What's up?" Stay focused on your intention and share your life's purpose and passions with others. It's the "be different" part of my motto. Say something that is going to have people remember you in a positive light. If you are having a down day, don't drag them down, and never forget to ask them "what's up" in their life. It's not all about you! If you do start by answering "what's up" first, you'll be surprised how many people search for something positive versus dropping the negative bomb in your lap.

People often feel obligated to have to stay there and listen to them vent and help them in some sort of way. If you get that bomb dropped, I highly recommend that you offer a follow up time to discuss so it doesn't ruin your evening (since their evening is already ruined) unless of course, they are your evening. You can also ask them, "What do you plan to do next?" More often than not, they can't or have no desire to fix what is broken. Some people are just not coachable and you need to decide what value they hold in your life.

Thrive, Don't Just Survive

When I was 26 years old, I was recruited to go work for

Wells Fargo Educational Financial Services. At the time of the call, I was happy working for my alma mater, Gettysburg College, in their Admissions Office. I really didn't know what to expect from a head hunter except when she said I could make up to a six figure salary, I was all ears and wanted to learn more. At age 26, money was in my top ten core principles and bordered on making my top five. I could potentially make $70,000 more than I was making at the time. I decided to go for it!

What I learned eleven months later was that I was darn good in sales and marketing, but I was incredibly lonely and unfulfilled in my life. The sales team and my supervisor were amazingly supportive and trained me with the best. The money was rolling in by the tens of thousands and tons of opportunity awaited me in my near future, but my intuition was telling me it was not the right occupation for me. In month eleven, I ran into a former colleague at West Chester University. He informed me that he had an opening in their Admissions and Financial Aid Office and it would provide me the avenue to pursue my masters. I already had the admissions experience and I acquired a minimal amount of financial aid experience through working for Wells Fargo. I told them that I would come in for the interview and weigh my options.

I decided to take the job, forfeiting the $30,000 Wells Fargo bonus I would have collected in month twelve. Needless to say, everyone I spoke to, including my parents, thought I lost my mind. Wells Fargo didn't want to lose me, so they offered to pay for my degree and let me work part-time. I decided to follow my intuition and took the job offer at West Chester University!

The lesson I learned was that if I chose to chase the almighty dollar, I would have thrived monetarily, but simply survived both personally and professionally. I wasn't willing to continue down that path of unhappiness. It also confirmed that money wasn't in my top five core principles. Everything is tied into the first P—principles. Did I have second thoughts when the person who took my place at Wells Fargo thanked me for the awesome job I did, and that he was grateful for the bonus? Absolutely, but only for a split second, because I knew in my heart I was to be doing something grander that would eventually make a difference in companies, schools and organizations across the nation. When I took the job with the university, I continued to get lucrative offers from banking institutions, but I knew I was just being tested as I continued searching for my legacy that was yet to be uncovered.

After year one at the university, I felt my passion fading for the world of Admissions and Financial Aid. I was working on my Masters in Training and Organizational Development at the time. I could have continued to survive, but what I did instead was find ways to keep my passion burning. I offered workshops on "I'm Important, You're Important, We're All Important" and began to develop training manuals and workshops for other areas within the division. Because of my thriving and taking on additional responsibilities, others took note of my new found skills and abilities. They went as far as to take me out of my current capacity and give me a trial run as their HR Training and Development Specialist. To date, I continue to serve as their Senior Intenal Consultant and follow my passions to inspire others to thrive, not only survive.

As you continue on your journey, you are going to be tested along the way. This is good. It means you are actually doing something right! You are living life. Always remember to align your principles and your passions, and your intuition will guide you the rest of the way. This is not to say that there won't be bumps along the way, but know there are lessons to be learned and shared with others so that they can benefit from your wisdom and experiences.

Aspire to Excel

When I was in middle school and high school, my dad and I would travel to his baby shoe factory every Saturday morning. I can remember being thirteen years old helping the women trim the shoes of imperfections; sometimes I even got to work in packing and shipping. That was a real treat! No matter what the job, I learned so many valuable lessons on those Saturday mornings. It was not uncommon for my dad to pop in motivational tapes in the car by Zig Ziglar and Tony Robbins. Not realizing what he was doing at the time, he was priming my mind to make a difference in this world. Sure there were some Saturdays that I didn't want to go into work, even though I only had to work from 6 until 11:30. Looking back now, that time in the car was my only real one-on-one time with my dad— driving to and from work on Saturday mornings.

I learned early that working in a factory was not my calling, but I also valued the incredible people my dad had working for him, and what joy they found in their life no matter what position they held in the company. At times I thought I was learning too much for my age, but I came to know that my experience in that factory was simply guiding me to build character and refining my social skills. I remember working with a partner to complete a case of shoes. We would each take a board filled with 24 pairs of shoes. We would trim the shoes and then put a secure-tatch and price tag on each pair. It seemed forever for me to get a board of shoes finished, but I would watch my partner, try it her way, and then I would adapt it and see how I could improve my own personal time without sacrificing my quality of work. I would play upbeat music that would help me to find my "groove." I figured if I have to be working on a Saturday morning, I might as well make the most of my time. Who would have predicted that 15 years later I would receive a Lean Six Sigma certificate from Villanova University where the focus is on process improvement and efficiency?

When the book *7 Habits of Highly Effective People* hit the book shelves, my dad said it was a "must read." Although my dad did not enjoy reading, he did read books aligned with making his business better. He was the bread winner. His goal was to be successful, so he could provide for his family. What he never focused on was not being able to provide. His family's happiness fueled his desire to succeed. As I mentioned earlier, he came from a farm family where he was the oldest of eleven. When he was asked to take over a failing shoe company, his experiences growing up in a large family, knowing the meaning of hard work, serving as an Army Reserve officer, and his incredible mechanical skills served him well.

My dad was about to help a well educated owner of a company live his dreams, and my dad, with no college degree, was going to be rewarded for his hard work. He became president of the baby shoe company. "Begin with the end in mind" was one of Steven Covey's habits that has always stuck in my head and in my dad's. The leadership skills and shrewd business knowledge he was acquiring was going to be what paid for my sister's and my college education. Not knowing we would both choose Gettysburg College, a highly selective private college only thirty minutes from home, he was going to provide us the education of our choice. While my mother focused on, "darn I should have gotten a job there so that I could have gotten their educations paid for," my father took it as an opportunity to serve on their parent boards, get involved and make a difference.

My father served as an exceptional role model for me in my formative years. Although he will be the first to admit he is not perfect (who is?), he will say that his role in life was to leave the world a better place, give his children what he didn't have, serve the Lord, and enjoy life. When I went off to college he advised me to hold onto my principles, and told me that after college is when I will really get my education. I never understood the second part until I experienced it first hand. I thought college was going to be the vehicle that would prepare me for everything. Although Gettysburg prepared me as well as they could, there was so much more to learn.

Aspiring to excel required me to not only to succeed, but to fail; not only feel loved, but also experience loneliness; to discover fulfillment, but also feel emptiness. The failures and feelings of loneliness are almost more powerful teachers than success and experiencing happiness. On your journey to aspiring to excel, you will open yourself up and show vulnerability and humility at times, but a true leader will make the extra effort to take others on that journey so that they too can learn and grow.

CHAPTER TWO: PASSION

STAR POWER ACTIONS

1.) Write down five things that have happened in your life that you wrote off as "coincidences." Assess them and try to draw connections as to why you think they happened. What was their purpose, and how were they connected to other events that may have happened in your life?

2.) Write down five intentions you would like to see happen in your life. Develop them into affirmations using the eight tips of attracting what you want out of life.

3.) Watch Randy Pausch's Last Lecture or read his book "The Last Lecture." Ask yourself what you would include in your lecture if you knew it was your last. Outline your legacy journey. If you are not satisfied with your current legacy, write it as if you are living the legacy you were intended to live. See how many of your intentions come true.

4.) Watch Anita Renfroe's YouTube Parody, "Mom's Song," to the William Tell Overature. Laugh it off and pass it on! Laughter is good for the soul. Make up your own parody to a song of your choice. Watch mine on my Legacy Producer YouTube Channel called "Oh Legacy."

5.) What visual and auditory signs can you surround yourself with to help you discover and ignite your passions?

6.) How can you help others live their passions? By helping others, you can share in their joy and successes. It can also enlighten you about your dreams, intentions, and future direction.

7.) Think about the most miserable person you know. Do you share any of their traits? How long would you like to spend face to face time with them? How are you going eliminate these traits and by when?

8.) Do you have a presence that people want to be around? What positive qualities do you possess? How do they translate into a positive presence? People do business with people they like, not necessarily because of what you sell.

9.) When someone asks you, "What's up?" do you have a good answer? Share your passions and your future desires with others.

10.) People want to be around positive, happy, future seeking people with a vision, and if they don't appreciate these qualities in you, ask yourself, "What is their purpose for them being in your life?" If you can't find an answer, you know what you need to do!

11.) Find truth tellers and have them answer the five questions mentioned under "Inspire Others with Your Presence." Assess them and plan specific changes that will happen as a result of their feedback. Share with them your plans and ask for them to be an accountability partner. Change is not always easy.

12.) Think about a time when you had a tough decision to make, what was it that made you choose what you did? What lessons did you learn from it, and how are you a better person because of it?

"Many people have a wrong idea of what constitutes true happiness. It is not attained through self-gratification but through fidelity to a worthy purpose"
–Helen Keller, American author and political activist

No. 3
PEOPLE

Establish Your Oikos

I hired an outside leadership consultant to come to West Chester University to speak. David had a very profound, uplifting voice that could both calm and excite you at the same time. After that, I never quite met someone who had that vibrato. Two days before he came to speak, I was flipping through the television channels and I heard a voice similar to his. I remember thinking to myself, "Well, that's bizarre" and flipped back to the religious channel that was playing a re-run of a movie he was in when he was in his early 30's. Was it a sign, and a sign for what?

He and I recently reconnected when he was in town doing some consulting work. I shared with him how his story of "oikos" had resonated with me, and how I would like to incorporate it into being part of my Last Sermon Project, where I help members of a congregation reflect on their legacy they have chosen to live. At the end of the program, they deliver a sermon as if it would be the last time they were to deliver a message to their congregation. In our conversation, this gentleman continued to share with me that one of his biggest audiences are churches, and that he enjoys doing work with them. Was it coincidence? Perhaps. Nevertheless, I paid close attention because the layout of the Molly Sunshine Tour was inspired by the Women of Faith Conference I attended three years ago at the Wachovia Center in Philadelphia. A bank manager randomly asked me to go after setting up my bank account for MyInternshipGopher.com. I never met her before in my life and now we are friends and still continue to go together every year.

Could it be a sign for something yet to come? I did tell a few people in my oikos that my vision is to one day present to large audiences across the nation starting with the Wachovia Center. Now you may be wondering what is "oikos?" In ancient Greek, oikos is equivalent to household or family. An oikos can also consist of friends, mentors, guardians, advisors, teachers, or any one else you choose to spend the most of your time with—it's your inner circle. The consultant was honored to have me reflect the story of oikos in my work, but I felt he was a messenger with a greater purpose. He came from higher education (like me), and began to explain the challenges of going into the consulting and speaking field on your own, especially given the current economic climate. The last piece of advice he gave me was I need to make sure I don't lose focus on what matters most in life. The whole way home I pondered David's last statement. What does matter most in life? What he was asking me to do was to reflect on my principles and passions. Are they in alignment?

David came back into my life at a very important time because my marriage was falling apart from all my outside adventures. My husband knew I had to put in the hours to get the businesses off the ground, but he was also growing tired of my having evening commitments, him running the house, the time he was putting in raising our child alone, while he too had a full time job. He was growing increasingly unhappy, and so was I. It became clear why David entered my life. He was reminding me that

I need to re-establish my oikos.

After assessing my oikos, I discovered that it was filling up with older successful business men, and was missing a balance of gender, age, and experience. My principles began to shift and I was hanging with people who had money in their top five core principles, which is fine; however, I began to sacrifice the happiness of my family. Knowing that I am the average of the ten people I spend the most time with, I knew I had to add more family-focused, successful women into my oikos, and I did!

To get the best out of your oikos, I sometimes recommend the Six Thinking Hats technique. More detailed information can be found at www.mindtools.com. In general, Edward de Bono's Six Thinking Hats is a powerful technique that helps people look at important decisions from a number of different perspectives. It helps people make better decisions by pushing them to move outside their habitual ways of thinking. In addition, it helps them understand the full complexity of a decision, and spot issues and opportunities which they might otherwise not have seen.

Many successful people think from a very rational, positive point-of-view. Often though, they may fail to look at problems from an emotional, intuitive, creative or negative vantage point. This can mean that they underestimate resistance to change, don't make creative leaps, and fail to make essential contingency plans. Similarly, pessimists may be excessively defensive, and people who are used to a very logical approach to problem solving, may fail to engage their creativity or listen to their intuition.

If you look at a problem or opportunity using the Six Thinking Hats technique, then the people in your oikos will use all of these approaches to develop the best solution. You will find that your decisions and plans that came from using the Six Thinking Hats will have a mix of ambition, skill in execution, sensitivity, creativity and have a good contingency planning. In other words, it is a plan that will help you live your legacy and make a difference!

Combat Energy Zappers

When reading about some of the energy zappers I have encountered over the years, I encourage you to think about the people in your life who may exhibit some of these energy-zapping characteristics. Think about how you have chosen to combat your energy zappers and assess what adaptations you may have to make in order to keep your 5 P's aligned. Often people focus on the other person's behaviors. I suggest that you start with what is in your control first. There will always be a few people who we cannot take out of our oikos for various reasons. In addition, many energy zappers are not willing to change their negative ways; however, we do have control as to how we react to them.

I remember on my first day of work, a co-worker who I was going to work closely with said, "I give you six months and you are going to be as frustrated and miserable as the rest of us." I thought to myself, "What did I do? Why did I take this job?" But then I quickly shifted to, "What can I do to make it better so that I'm not frustrated and miserable in six months?" I told her that I was up for the challenge and began to put together my own trainer's manual so the next person would have a shorter learning curve.

Although I wasn't able to change her attitude, I respected her for her knowledge and experience. She started working at the university right after high school, 25 years ago. She is no longer with us, but I do have a beautiful painting she painted for my husband and I as a wedding gift in our bedroom. Although she was an energy zapper and she knew it, I made sure that it wasn't my energy she was zapping. I would make comments like, "I see you are having another great day! What can I do to make it better?" It brought awareness to her behaviors. All energy zappers are not that easy to control. She and I developed a very special relationship. We accepted each other for who we were, not who we wish the other would be.

I had another energy zapper in my professional career. While working in higher education, I had a boss whose entire life revolved around his job and would be best described as a micromanager who was stuck in the 70's style of doing business. He didn't seem to have many friends, had a broken family, never was married, and had no children. From what I gathered, all he had was his job. In addition, no one ever appropriately addressed his debilitating leadership style over the years; this behavior was either overlooked due to his long hours and "loyalty," or because they did not see it because he put on a good game face to those above him.

I remember one time in the office kitchen he said out loud, "Employees are replaceable. They come and go in this line of business." Probably not the best choice of words, especially given one of his new staff members was in the kitchen trying to enjoy her lunch. I guess you can't teach some energy zappers how to zap less life out of people. Employees would cringe at his voice and would find ways to look busy as he walked down the hall to people's offices to see how their work was progressing and plop down to complain about other employees in the office. Yep! This is a real, live person and perhaps you know of someone similar.

You may be wondering how I survived this situation. No matter what job I take on, I take pride in my work and focus on the people who benefit from my services. In this case, it wasn't him. Sure, my work was a direct reflection on him, but for me to sabotage my own success would be in direct conflict with my principles. It would only attract more negative energy. As long as upper administration wasn't going to see the signs, listen to the employees, or do anything about it, I was going to work on an exit strategy, and I did. To this day, he is still allowed to drain employees of their creative energy and passion. I encourage you to not stay in an energy draining situation for too long. Your self-esteem and vision can become distorted and crushed.

When I started my career at the university, there was a gentleman who was there for 30 years. I launched a professional development program within his division, while still working in a different capacity at the university. Not ever having met me, he proceeded to write me a two page e-mail about my wanting to climb the ladder to a promotion, and that this organization doesn't need professional development, and who am I to think I can provide it? I did something that probably most people had never done to him in the past. I picked up the phone to have a conversation with him. Needless to say, he was surprised to receive my call, and by the end of the conversation, he was very apologetic. Did he change? Maybe... Maybe not. However, what I can only hope is that he will think twice before sending a flaming e-mail.

Another energy zapper I met was considered aloof in the office environment. She didn't have to say a word, but she made others feel uncomfortable. Remember the energy I spoke about earlier? If it doesn't feel right, there's probably meaning behind it. At one time she even said to me that she didn't trust me and that "her grandmother once said that one should only speak when spoken to." To that I said, "Can you please explain what I have done for you not to trust me?" You could hear a pin drop and then she said "I just don't." Later on I realized that my happiness and my *perceived* "lack of baggage" (her words) was a trigger for her. People come with their own clutter, and it goes back to "you are who you are in spite of or because of" as I indicated in the first chapter.

You have a choice in life as to how you are going to react to situations. Was I going to withdraw and keep my ideas to myself knowing that they might better the department? What do you think? Was I going to act like the sky was falling and life was miserable because someone's done me wrong? NO WAY! Dealing with the energy zappers is equally important as dealing with those who are going to help you live your dreams. There is such a thing as healthy conflict. Get comfortable about being uncomfortable, especially when others need help seeing how they are treating others, even when it is you.

The last energy zapper story I will mention happened early in my career and could have changed my entire career path. An associate director decided to sit in on one of my information sessions where I would share with students and parents what the college had to offer. I'm a lively, engaging presenter. I've always enjoyed presenting, and have won speech competitions at an early age. To that end, I had a past governor say, "I'll see you on Broadway." Although I am not on Broadway, I still like to give people not only information they need, but also be able to process it in an engaging manner. After my presentation, I overheard the associate director say to a co-worker that my presentation felt like a Saturday Night Live skit.

Being the assertive women I am, I followed up with her and said thank you for the feedback and asked her what she would recommend I change. Again, complete silence. I even offered for her to come back once she had time to think about it. Because of my own emotional intelligence, I ended up tracking the students who matriculated from that session to the university and there was a 60% matriculation, and thank you cards addressing how great the session was compared to their other experiences. Think about what would have happened if I went back to giving dull information seminars to these parents and students. It might have affected the overall number of students matriculating to that university.

Why did I share all these negative stories? Because there are lessons to be learned from them, and it goes back to my core mission of "make a difference, be the difference!" You can't chase stars in the sunshine if you are stuck hanging in the rain clouds. When something bad happens, look for the positive lessons to be learned. In addition, the more positive energy you put out to the world, the more success and rewards you will receive. Don't focus on the negative and place judgment on others. You might become an energy zapper for someone else. When you approach life with a positive attitude, it may increase the frequency of energy zappers trying to shoot darts at your ideas or positive approach to life. I've had people tell me to stop being so happy, people will think I'm fake. Nevertheless, focus on how you can strengthen your shield so that the darts don't penetrate your 5 P's. You have control over how you react to them. Keep your principles, passions and people in alignment. You will only gain more momentum, strength, and confidence in your journey. Trust the universe and move forward!

So far I have addressed your energy zappers. I know it is hard to believe, but there are those who may say you zap their energy. For example, there are those who would see me as a driven, assertive, passionate, happy, and kind-hearted woman. On the flip side, there are others who may see me as aggressive, unreasonable, fake, exhausting, and self-centered. How can this be? They come from a difference frame of reference. In other words, we are blessed to be a part of a world where people come from different cultural backgrounds, geographical locations, education, values, religion, race, age, gender, and have different life experiences. As a result, you are given a choice to see these differences as blessings or a curse. I encourage you to seek the high road!

For you not to become an energy zapper to others, you must be cognizant of people's frame of reference and adapt your style where you can. At next year's Molly Sunshine Tour, I plan to launch my second book called, *Crazy Eights: If You Can't Beat Them, Join Them*. It outlines eight distinct personality styles and strategies on how to adapt given the situation and personality style you encounter. The sooner we realize the importance of effective communication and practice adapting our style, the sooner we stop zapping other people's energy and get our ideas heard and accepted. The best way to get your 5 P's out of alignment is to zap other people's energy or allow ourselves to be zapped. How we react to a situation or person is in our control. Make wise choices!

Drawing Lines in the Sand

It is natural that we go from energy zappers to drawing lines in the sand. Often we allow others to draw lines in the sand and set our expectations. Just think what would have happened to my current career if I chose to become a dull and drab presenter. I wouldn't have a career in motivating and equipping people of all ages to live their legacies by helping them to develop new skills, grow into a person they love, giving them the confidence to share their dreams with others.

What happens when you draw a line in the sand and the tide comes in? It washes away, right? Sometimes there are people who draw the line in the sand and then keep moving it to have some type of power over you. Sometimes people think that they are doing you a favor by giving you all their guidance without allowing you to think for yourself. Sometimes you forget to draw your own line in the sand, and no matter what you do, it isn't good enough. After all, thinking, planning, failing and succeeding is all a part of living your legacy. If you don't fail, you're not doing. If you fail to achieve, you fail to try.

These are a few of the reflection questions that have helped me keep my 5 P's aligned. As you read the following stories, here are a few questions I would like you to consider asking yourself.

1. What lines in the sand have been drawn for you over the years? Were they helpful? How did they limit your success?

2. What lines do you need to draw in the sand today so that others don't try to draw them for you?

3. In the past, what positive resulted from people's potentially hurtful words?

4. Have you drawn any lines in the sand that are limiting you to reach your full potential?

When I said I wanted to get my Masters in Training and Organizational Development, my father said it is "fluff" and it is the first thing that companies cut when times get tough. First of all, it can be "fluff" if learning outcomes are not measured, and yes, I know it is the first thing to get cut. I could have said to myself, "He's being a jerk" or choose to see that my father was trying to protect me and he means no harm. It's like my mother saying you are crazy to leave a job unless you have another job with *good* health benefits. My mother has health problems so again, she was just trying to protect me based on her experiences. Another powerful example was after I gave birth to Tyler. When my mother found out that my delivery was "easy," she said, "My God, I hope that doesn't mean you are going to have another one." What she meant to say was that two is a lot of work and that children cost a lot of money.

What people say is not always what they mean. We have our own filters that can distort a person's intended message. Look for the opportunity to reframe people's messages even when they are intended to hurt you. At times, we need to assess if what they are saying is helpful. Other times, we need to ask for further clarification, but at all times, you need to listen to your intuition. Sure you might fail or be disappointed, but know that your next success could be right around the corner. Don't ever stop setting your own expectations and drawing your own lines in the sand!

Help Others Join the Shift

Wayne Dwyer came out with a movie recently called *The Shift*. It was produced by Hay House, and I highly recommend you watch the movie. I'm not sure how I even got onto Hay House's mailing list, but am glad that I did. They are a publisher dedicated to helping others join the shift of getting the world back on track and focused on goodness. Louise Hay, owner of Hay House, has a mission similar to my own, and everyone she associates with seems to have the same mission in life—heal from within and live an abundant life. One day, my goal is to have Hay House publish one of my books.

A week after I wrote my children's book, *A Tale of Miss Molly Sunshine*, I attended a Hay House event at the Philadelphia Convention Center with my husband. In the back of the room there was a table full of products being sold, one was of Louise Hay's children's book titled *I Think I Am*. Could it have been a sign? Perhaps, but you bet I bought it! I'll figure out why when the opportunity presents itself to me.

My personal shift began when I met one particular individual approximately three years ago. We immediately connected on a level that at the time I could not really explain. After that, I began to attract more individuals with similar energies. It almost was if by our paths crossing, more greatness followed—situations, opportunities, and people. I also began attracting people into my life who needed guidance. They were seeking purpose, meaning and fulfillment. I discovered not only that I had a gift, but also there were people who made good money coaching others.

At the time, my supervisor at West Chester University had recently received his coaching certificate and he shared with me some of the coaching strategies he was learning. Although I do not have my official certification, I was reassured by the strategies he would share. It was very similar to my approach to coaching my clients. In my "you must give to receive" attitude, I gifted a Last Sermon Project and a Coffee with the Rhinos program. Each program yielded a coaching client that synergized with my essence. They were simply a little lost in their journey. They reached their initial goals, and continued to establish and reach new heights. In addition, they found a sense of purpose and passion they hadn't felt for a very long time. Sure, life still throws them curveballs, but they now know how to hit them out of the ballpark. I continue to attract the clients I choose to help live their legacy. I'm helping people join "the shift" and find fulfillment in life.

Having said this, I always wanted to develop a company where I would be able to help people, organizations and schools "produce legacies." The client would choose which "Legacy Adventure" they are interested in living through my coaching, consulting, training, or production business! It is their journey. I simply help them layout and achieve their Legacy Action Plan depending on the adventure they chose. I come from a philosophy that if you can dream it, you can do it, but you also must believe it and commit to your dreams with constant thoughts, planning and actions. If you are interested in learning more about my Legacy

Producers company go to *www.LegacyProducers.com.*

I encourage you to discover how you can help others join the shift. I'm not saying that you need to go out and become a coach or build a company around helping others discover their life's purpose and strategies to live up to their full potential. What I am suggesting is that you consciously look for ways to help and inspire others. Give others encouragement, look outside yourself, give of your gifts, help a neighbor, set goals to give of your money or time to non-profits or organizations you would like to support. By helping others join the shift and other people's missions, you will begin to live in the world of abundance and will spend less time focusing on what is missing in your life. Gratitude will be placed upon you and those you come in contact with. It supports the tried but true saying that you got to give to receive. If you have children ages 4-6, I highly recommend that you read this book to your children, *Tyler's Tidal Wave Adventure*. I wrote the book with this adage in mind–"We not only need to model the way for others, but also for those who are most impressionable, our young children!"

Align the Three P's

Principles, passion, and people are tightly linked. If one is out of alignment, the universe and situations in your life will be sure to let you know. Of course there will always be certain things that happen out of your control; however, principles, passion and people are the foundation that will help you to *persist* and develop a sense of *peace*—the final two P's to *Chasing Stars*! Aligning the three P's is definitely an art. It requires you to look deep inside, ask the tough questions, and gain the skills necessary to not only dream, but also prepare for the next opportunity that presents itself. Five years ago I wouldn't have predicted that I would gain the knowledge on how to build websites, develop e-newsletters, effectively use social media, write self achievement and children's books, compose and record songs with a Grammy-winning artist, build brands, market three companies, launch a product line and go on tour, all while raising a five year old and working full time in three short years.

I don't tell you this to brag, but to show you that the only difference between the words impossible and possible is the meaning you give to them. What started the shift? Five years ago, I made a conscious effort to discover and explore my true passions, my core principles became clearer, and I began aligning myself with the people who had common interests, persistence, passion and principles. In other words, the people who already had their five P's to living their dreams in action! No one ever said life was easy, but it's those who do nothing who will always get what they always have gotten. Although five years ago I didn't know what my future looked like in totality, I did feel I was being called to help women, young children, and students achieve their dreams, clear the mental clutter, and spark creativity and innovation.

I mentioned earlier that one of my major mantras I use to guide my life is from Steven Covey's *7 Habits of Highly Effective People*, "Begin with the end in mind." I always had a vision of what the end looked like, but it was figuring out the "how, when, and where." Don't forget— five years ago I had just given birth to a beautiful baby boy who rightfully commanded my attention. When Tyler reached two years old, I started to get the itch to discover what it was that I was ultimately being called to do. I thoroughly enjoy my job at West Chester University, but knew that there would eventually come a time when I would need to prepare for my ultimate goal—to inspire women, children and young adults, throughout the world to be prepared for what life had to offer them—in other words, helping them shift into their own greatness!

I encourage you to look at your three P's—Principles, Passions, and People. How well are they aligned? What does your "end" look like? If you don't make the time to search, discover, and share with others what your possible "end" looks like, it will take that much longer to realize what it is you are supposed to be doing. Don't look for the "perfect" life or solution. Look at the things that matter most to you and see what you can do to strengthen them starting today. You might want a better job, a stronger relationship with your spouse, less debt, more time with your children. Whatever it is, you need to begin with the end in mind and start taking steps every day towards that goal. Start aligning your three P's with concrete star power actions today!

STAR POWER ACTIONS

1.) List the top 10 people in your oikos. How do you feel about who is in your oikos? Who would you like to add? Who do you need to eliminate?

2.) What are you doing that is helping you take care of your whole being? What habits do you need to eliminate or adapt to become a "well being" both in mind, body and soul?

3.) Who are the energy zappers in your life? Who do you need to eliminate? Where can you adapt your style of communication? What is your plan and when will you accomplish your goals?

4.) What lines in the sand are currently being drawn in the sand for you? Who is drawing them and is there a good reason why they are the ones drawing the line? Do you have your own set of expectations for yourself? How do you know when you are being successful?

5.) Are you currently experiencing a discomfort in where you are? Why? Are you experiencing a shift? What are you currently doing about it? What are you doing to find fulfillment and happiness in life? Who or what do you need to take action? Is there anything small you can do to start forward motion?

6.) Are there people around you who are currently in "the shift?" Do you know the difference between someone who is complaining and others who may be experiencing "growing pains?" What can you do to help them through their shift? How do you feel helping others through the shift will positively affect you?

7.) How is your alignment of the 3 P's—Principles, Passion, and People? Do you need a tune-up? Where and how much is it going to cost you? In other words, what do you have to lose/gain as a result of re-aligning the 3 P's?

"Never doubt that a small group of thoughtful committed citizens can change the world. Indeed, it is the only thing that ever has."

-Margaret Mead, American cultural anthropologist

No. 4
PERSISTENCE

Hold the Vision

There are so many things that can take you off your path to living your dreams and achieving your goals. It is important to clarify your vision and be able to adapt when the unexpected happened. Throughout my career in higher education, it was becoming clear that many students were graduating from college without a sense of purpose and sometimes direction. It seemed that many were going through the motions and simply looking for the means to the end. In other words, get a college degree and then figure out what they want to do with their life after that. I guess you may have put me in that category too. I was able to graduate with psychology and elementary education degrees with hands on experience; however, it wasn't until my student teaching experience that I felt that it wasn't what I was supposed to be doing despite all of my success.

At the end of my senior year in college, I received the student teacher of the year award. In addition, fifteen years later, I still have students from my student teaching classroom who keep in touch and recount some of the fun activities we did in the classroom. Do I have regrets in my decision not to go into the classroom to teach? Absolutely not! I know that the direction I am heading will allow me to achieve my five year goal. You may have heard of a BHAG before—Big Hairy Audacious Goal. As I mentioned in an earlier chapter, my five year goal is to inspire 500,000 people of all ages and raise $500,000 dollars by 2015.

While my sister, mother and I were sitting at one of my parent's favorite Italian restaurants, I asked them the question, "What do you think I feel is more important, money or serving others?" Prior to anyone answering, I was thinking "serving others." My mother responded, "Definitely serving others." My sister quickly said, "No way. Molly wants to make money." My mother looked confused and so did I. Julie continued to explain that "The more money Molly makes, the more she will give away and make an even bigger difference." I have no idea what possessed me to ask this question of them, but it led me to go from my one company, MyInternshipGopher.com, to searching for more opportunities. I realized that schools still have barriers up that will prevent MyInternshipGopher.com to take off and really make an impact, so I went back into the universe searching for more clues.

When I gave Dave Magrogan my My Internship Gopher business card with a cartoon gopher staring straight at him, he knew I was different. When he asked me "What's up?" he immediately wanted to learn more, and after he gave his keynote at that chamber luncheon, he noted that he could feel my energy and passion from the stage. It is important to wear your principles and passions on the outside. Don't hold them in where no one will see them except you. Although MyInternshipGopher.com wasn't growing as fast as I had hoped, I saw another opportunity and created the vision of a motivational speaking and training group called *Rhino Living*. He loved it and allowed me to run with it. He trusted me and knew we shared similar passions. "Give Love Serve" is one of Dave's personal mottos. I decided to put myself out there and work for free, and own a share of the company. My father, the baby boomer, was concerned that I was getting "taken advantage of." I assured him that what I was learning was worth so much more than money, and that one day, what I have learned and the people I have met through *Rhino Living* will help make me fulfill in totality my life's mission to make a difference and be the difference.

You must have the strength to hold the vision! Keep in mind, people who give this type of advice often have the best of intentions. They are not trying to take you off your path. They are simply making sure that you have thought things through. It also tests your passion and helps your vision and direction gain clarity.

One of my mentors often said, "Why don't you do it (form your own training company) for yourself?" I told him that my intuition was telling me to wait. I felt I had more lessons to learn and experiences to gain. This is the same mentor who told me, "If you have an idea, start a company and start building. Some of your companies will carry the others that may fail." Most people probably would have thought that was nutty advice, but it has worked for me. Don't be afraid to try out different philosophies and approaches to life, leadership and entrepreneurism.

I also didn't want to start my own training company yet because I wanted to have a different story to tell— something spectacular—My own "Legacy Story!" I was confident in my ability to move people to action through my speaking abilities and the areas of expertise; however, I felt I had more to learn from the experts such as Tony Robbins, Jack Canfield, and Dave Magrogan. I wanted to know what made them millionaires and a success in business. In addition, it felt like one out of every ten people I met was a motivational speaker, trainer, or consultant. Given this economy, I wanted to provide something different—the Molly Sunshine Tour certainly achieved that goal. Founding a tour like this and being on stage with celebrity speakers certainly was a fabulous way to break into new markets and make a difference.

When I was in my twenties, my dad once told me that I couldn't be a motivational speaker. He commented, "What do I have to tell people that would be of interest to them?" I remember thinking, why do I have to have some tragic story to tell in order to be a motivational speaker? I still choose not to focus on the challenges life has given me, but how I was able to overcome them. After all, my name is Molly Sunshine. I choose to focus on the sunnyside of life, and I want to encourage others to do the same.

As you know, life is full of ups and downs. It's your choice on whether you prefer to focus on the obstacles or on the small wins and people who can help you achieve your dreams. With MyInternshipGopher.com I could have chosen to focus on the teachers who didn't have time or were hesitant to try something new, or I could focus on the parents who desperately seek something like this for their children. I realized I needed to gain the superintendent's buy-in and teacher support for Gopher to get digging. I know that in 2015, MyInternshipGopher.com will have its place in our schools and it will help high school aged children get acclimated to the world of work, explore careers, and find mentors in the workforce prior to going to college. My hope is that they will find more meaning in what they choose to study and our workforce will benefit from it in the end.

Being aware of my other vision to inspire women and children of all ages, I knew I had more to give than MyInternshipGopher.com. At the time, I was president of two companies, working full time at West Chester University, and being a mother to our son and a wife to my husband. It was quite the challenge. However, I felt it was time for me to write my story and launch my message. What started out as a one-person book launch, turned out to be an eight star-powered speaker line-up in a beautiful garden venue. Once I announced the tour, developed yet another website, blog and social media accounts, I knew I was onto something great. The vibrations were high and over the next five months, I attracted the people (*one of the five P's*) I needed to make it a success, and discovered fabulous opportunities for some of the people already traveling on a similar journey with similar passions.

Having already developed my keynote and interactive workshop that outlined what would be my book, I knew I also needed to develop a train the trainer program. Someone who works closely with Ken Blanchard advised me that if family is one of my top five core principles, I must develop a train the trainer program so that others can convey my *Chasing Stars in the Sunshine* message to the masses. Having facilitated nationally known train the trainer programs such as, *The Fish Philosophy, Who Moved My Cheese, Whale Done,* and fine-tuned the *Rhino Living* program for schools and a Coffee with the Rhinos program for businesses, I knew this was a natural next step, especially if I wanted to keep my principles and passions aligned.

I also knew I needed a book! Since Dave and I wrote *Do It Rhino Style* in fifteen days, I figured writing my own book should be a walk in the park. Having said this, you have to have confidence, believe in yourself, and surround yourself with the people who have taken it to the next level. Holding onto the vision also requires you to seek out advice from the best in the industry. As a result, I also took Peggy McColl's class on how to get on the best seller list and participated in Jack Canfield's Business Success Principles workshop. When I shared with Jack Canfield my five year goal of $500,000 and 500,000 people, I asked him, "When do you know you need a PR agent?" He replied, "When you ask that question." That is exactly what I wanted to hear. It gave me the fuel I needed to keep on moving forward and quickly with my five year goal.

On the day my husband and I were traveling up to Boston to experience Jack Canfield's Success Principles Workshop, I was connected with a PR agent who wanted to book speaker events at Dave Magrogan's restaurants, and also wanted to book him as a keynote speaker in September. I inquired about which client Leslie Padilla was representing. It just so happened that the week before, there was a person from that same company trying to connect with me. Signs are everywhere. Make the connections!

What happened next was absolutely amazing. I came to discover that Leslie also represents Lynn Doyle from CN8 in Philadelphia. I had three spots left on the tour and Leslie and I shared amazing synergy. She also represents Ashley Cook, the editor of Phlare Magazine. Lynn, Leslie and Ashley took the last three spots on the Molly Sunshine Tour. They joined me, Beth Strange, an image consultant who recently wrote a book with Steven Covey, Tracy Davidson from NBC10, and Dave Magrogan, restaurateur, serial entrepreneur, and business partner with Rhino Living.

I can go on and on; however, you get the point. It takes persistence, passion, and people to help you hold onto your vision. The Molly Sunshine Tour turned out even more magical than I could have ever imagined. There are always going to be things that don't go your way. Let it go! Look for signs for future opportunities, make the connections, and be persistent. Focus on what is going well, not what may have gone wrong.

Prepare and Plan for Your Success

Many of the opportunities I mentioned in this chapter were not listed on the initial The Molly Sunshine Tour vision board. It went the same way for the business plan for MyInternshipGopher.com, Rhino Living and Legacy Producers. In my past, I thrived on structure and it served me well. However, when working on a project that is so new and in unchartered territory with a slight learning curve attached to it, there are going to be things you are going to want to shift. There are things that I have learned to let go and adapt; such as, holding onto every vision because I put so much time into it. So often it's not that the idea was bad, it was simply not the right time. Since I still enjoy structure, I have a place I put these ideas and revisit them quarterly. Some ideas have been in the folder for over a year. That's ok! Let it go! Look for how the projects fit into your mission and vision. If they don't fit now, they might fit later or perhaps not at all. I enjoy looking at some of the older ideas to celebrate how far I have come since the birth of that idea. See how you can use positivity to reframe the moment!

I also discovered that it is more fun when you have others collaborating with you on the vision. You can't always plan for that because you don't always know when you are going to meet people who want to be a part of the vision. Sometimes, if you stick too close to the plan, you may miss an opportunity or a person that could help you live your dreams. I never would have thought that I would have an extensive product line in development as I do unless I was keeping some of my goals loose enough to expand.

If you are just starting out in your journey, develop a plan that will cause you to take continuous action daily. Also, depending on the size of your project and your stakeholders, the scope and detail of your business plan may vary. If you are just getting started, one of my mentors highly recommended *The Art of the Start* by Guy Kawasaki. In his book he gives you a trick into how to write a business plan using power point in twelve slides or less. He also gives great advice that a business plan is never perfect. A good business plan is forever changing. There is no such thing as a perfect business plan. When you are 80% done, launch it and start building!

When developing anything, whether a company, product line, building a team, planning events, writing books, or problem solving, I've always used a popular process called mind mapping. Mind mapping is a diagram used to represent words, ideas, tasks, or other items linked to and arranged around a central key word or idea. I've used mind mapping in goal setting and achievement. It was made popular by Tony Buzan, a popular British psychology author. I like mind mapping using good old fashioned paper and colored markers. For those who are more linear, you might want to use flow charts. Use what produces the best results for you. The elements of a given mind map are arranged intuitively according to the importance of the concepts, and are classified into groupings, branches, or areas, with the goal of representing or other connections between portions of information.

According to Wikipedia, "Presenting ideas in a radial, graphical, non-linear manner, mind maps encourage a brainstorming approach to planning and organizational tasks. Though the branches of a mind map represent hierarchical tree structures, their radial arrangement disrupts the prioritizing of concepts typically associated with hierarchies presented with more linear visual cues. This orientation towards brainstorming encourages users to enumerate and connect concepts without a tendency to begin within a particular conceptual framework." Now that you know how it works, just don't think about it, do it!

I also encourage you to share your mind maps with others. People will be amazed at how you were able to think through multiple scenarios and visualize your current and future success. I remember showing my "six degrees of separation" drawing to one of my mentors for one of my companies. After seeing what I did, he introduced me to remote viewing which is a whole other subject. Basically, you bring attention to your intentions of the past and connecting them to your future which heightens the possibilities of things actually occurring. When mind mapping out a project, I use blue painters tape and post my mind maps to a wall in my guest room. I also post any signs that symbolize its success, and people I want to meet or have help in the project. All of these actions increase your intentions and help your dreams become your reality. It also requires you to always be searching for signs and opportunities, making the connections and expressing gratitude when you receive them. I have posted things on the wall that haven't come true until a few months later. Some are still posted from three years ago, but I realize a few of my small wins have to happen first for others to come true.

When I first started mind mapping MyInternshipGopher.com, I mapped out the entire processing system on the entire length of my basement wall. Before my business partner accepted the opportunity, he wanted to see what the system looked like. I invited him to see my mind maps in the basement. He was blown away and accepted the opportunity on the spot! Align the three P's and put persistence behind the idea. You will see that you too can make the impossible, possible!

Know the Difference between Tempters and Guardians

One of my professors in graduate school introduced us to the Hero's Journey. I probably should have learned it in high school, but it didn't have relevance until I was able to apply it to my own situation in life. The Hero's Journey is a way to put your head around change that is happening in your life. Whether the Satir Model or The Hero's Journey resonates more—just find one that resonates with you because the sooner you accept that change does not have a beginning and an end, the better off you will be. Accept that change is a continuous cycle. The more change you experience, the greater the potential you have of learning and growing exponentially. You not only build your resilience, but also prepare you for your future success. How well you manage change is how well you will succeed in life.

According to a Hero's Journey, you go through three main stages—the "departure" (leaving from what is known) to the "initiation" (the trial period and transformation) and finally, the "return" (integrating what was learned into every day life). Along the way you will be greeted by tempters—those who can lead you astray or take you off your path. You will also discover guardians who are there to help and guide you to your destination so that you arrive stronger and wiser. Prior to launching anything, even predevelopment, look for your tempters and guardians. Those who are successful anticipate who can help you in your journey and bring awareness to those who are looking to hinder your progress. Look how you can strengthen your relationships with allies and weaken your restraining forces.

In addition, tempters or guardians don't always have to take human form. It could be a policy or process that could corrupt or aid your future success. I sometimes use a powerful assessment tool called Force Field Analysis. The goal of this analysis is to identify forces for change and forces against change as it relates to your new plan or idea.

Once you have carried out this analysis, you can decide whether your project is viable. You might initially question whether it is worth going ahead with the plan or idea. Where you have already decided to carry out a project, Force Field Analysis can help you to work out how to improve its probability of success. Identify ways to reduce the strength of the forces opposing a project and ways to increase the forces pushing a project forward towards success. Often the most common solution people choose is just trying to force change; however that may cause its own problems. People can be uncooperative if change is forced on them. You also could be your own tempter. We will discuss this more in the final chapter.

Take a Fear Not Approach

It is not uncommon for me to jump in with both feet on some adventures, while other opportunities I stick my big toe in to see if the water is too hot or too cold. When it comes to money, I am definitely a big toe type of person. When it came to starting up three companies in three years or writing a book in fifteen days, I never hesitated. Instead, I just did it. When I was starting company number two, I remember volunteering at my son's vacation bible school. I don't know who benefited more—Tyler or me! Some of the messages were "fear not" and "I will not be afraid." It gave me the courage to keep on moving forward and living my legacy!

There was one thing that petrified me. Although I was fortunate to have a supervisor who supported my outside adventures, there were some people who were not as supportive. For the longest time, I was afraid to share my outside adventures because I was afraid that I would get penalized somehow, or worse, lose my job. It was fear based thinking. I also didn't want people to think what I was doing was "on the clock." As I mentioned under the "Energy Zapper" section of this book, people come from different frames of references that I have no control over. No matter what I say or do, some people will choose to see it from their own point of view. Having said this, for the longest time, I was still afraid of the false judgment that others might place upon me. It would potentially misalign my 5 P's and I didn't want to lose my positive momentum "to make a difference and be the difference."

Shortly after vacation bible school, I took my first step towards taking a "fear not approach" by volunteering to present the Art of Assertiveness to a Women's Leading Up student group on campus. For the first time, students and administrators heard my entrepreneur success story about living one's dreams and applying assertiveness to make a difference in the world. After that presentation, I began to receive more calls to present to groups, such as greek life, student government, and first year student orientation.

I soon began receiving calls from other universities—I was free, free at last! It felt great to speak freely and inspire others at my own University with my story of *Chasing Stars: The 5 P's to Living Your Dreams*, as well as others. As a result of my successes, I am able to help the University make new connections and my department benefits from my newly acquired knowledge. Looking back, I am thankful I decided to stick my big toe in first. As a result, I can freely share my experiences and help students, faculty and staff grow their strengths, shift their weaknesses, and instill in them the confidence they need to make the impossible, possible! Whether you take a total "fear not" approach, what matters most is that you are taking steps towards living your dreams and making a difference in this world. It's those who do nothing that we need to get moving in a forward motion. Take a step each day towards living your legacy. You'll be glad you did!

Seizing Opportunities

There are those who call me lucky. There are those who say I was in the right place at the right time, and others who simply say, "She's a go getter." I always like to refer to my-self as a "go-giver." When I built MyInternshipGopher.com,

I was asked to serve on a committee that encouraged entrepreneurism in teachers. At my first meeting I sat beside a man named Bob, who was a partner with a corporate training company. We hit it off immediately. A few months later he asked me to meet for breakfast with his friend, Steve, who has a book called *Conversations on Networking*. Bob wondered if I would be interested in meeting with them to explore the possibility of designing a training program that accompanies Steve's book. I'm always open to exploring opportunities that fit my principles and passions so I decided to take Bob up on the opportunity. Bob, Steve and I hit it off as a group, and when Bob left for another meeting, Steve and I continued to plan and talk for the next two hours. We even changed locations and had lunch. We both thought to ourselves, "What fun!"

Steve got busy with other serial entrepreneur types of things, as did Bob and I. A year later we came back together and thought the timing was right. Steve and I developed the program, and it is in the hands of Bob waiting for licensing. Did I mention this was another project I did for free? However, I will get a portion of the royalties once it is produced. Yes, another "sweat equity" project. However, what I later discovered is that Steve is a great mentor, friend, and had fascinating connections and served on a variety of boards. Steve was the one who knew the co-author of *The Last Lecture*, Jeffery Zaslow, Senior Editor at the *Wall Street Journal*. This was the inspiration behind my Legacy Producers business.

As a result of this experience, I learned a few big lessons about seizing opportunities. The timing has to be right. Patience is a virtue—*not just an overused expression*. Relationships are *more important* than the almighty dollar.

You decide what you value and where you want to spend your time. Whatever you do, I encourage you to follow your intuition, search for opportunities, and approach every opportunity with great optimism and confidence. *Carpe deim!*

CHAPTER FOUR: PERSISTENCE

STAR POWER ACTIONS

1.) What does success look like to you? What are some attributes that you have that will help you sustain your forward motion towards your future success?

2.) If you were to draw your first mind map, what idea or project would you map out?

3.) When implementing a new change, what are the forces that will help you move swiftly through the change and which things would hold you back?

4.) What are you going to do to weaken the restraining forces and strengthen the driving forces toward reaching your goal?

5.) Given a project or idea you are trying to implement, who are your guardians and tempters? What are you going to do to build your coalition of fans?

6.) What was the last project where you took a "fear not" approach? What lessons did you learn by taking this approach? Get comfortable about being uncomfortable.

7.) Remember a time when you seized an opportunity that crossed your path. What did it feel like? What opportunity is waiting to be seized? Is it aligned with your principles and passions? What people do you need to help you seize the opportunity? What is stopping you from acting on it?

"Far away there in the sunshine are my highest aspirations. I may not reach them, but I can look up and see their beauty, believe in them, and try to follow where they lead."

-Louisa May Alcott, American novelist,
best known for her book, Little Women

No. 5
PEACE

Positivity to the Power of Three (P³)
Positive Thoughts, Positive Actions and Positive Reframe

Fall in Love with Yourself Both Inside and Out

Growing up, I recall my mother saying things like, "Wear lipstick. You look like death warmed over." Literally, I had no idea what she was talking about, but figuratively it spoke to me, "I am ugly without makeup." She would also make comments when she thought my bottom was getting too big, or my thighs getting too jiggly. We've all been told something negative about our physical image, but depending on how we interpret the words, it could shatter our self-esteem and future dreams.

While growing up, my parents encouraged my sister and me to dream. With that, our confidence grew inside of us. I also realized that the words that my mother chose to use were words she probably heard as a child. My mother struggles with her weight and is in poor health. She reminds me often that she never weighed what I weigh until in her 40's. I could have processed her words as "that means I'll end up being obese," or "I'll weigh 140 for the rest of my life." I've weighed 140 for the past 20 years, who's to say I won't weigh 140 for the next 20 years? Me, that's who! Eliminate your self-limiting beliefs.

It's that confidence that has allowed me to overcome hurtful language that I have heard over the years. Learning how to effectively reframe people's words and actions into something positive and by looking at the situation from their frame of reference takes time and patience to develop. My mother's intentions were out of love and based on her own experiences growing up. She wanted me to look my best and make a good impression. Having said this, while I did care about my outside appearance, I also cared about my inside appearance. Growing up I had emotional highs and lows. To this day, I often joke with my mother that I'm surprised she didn't put me up for adoption in my teen years. It was that journey to finding love for myself that was the toughest growing up. I always thought my older sister was the pretty one. Looking back on pictures, neither one of us was that good looking; however, today I have learned to *feel* beautiful both inside and out by focusing on the 5 P's!

I always have tried to find love in my heart so I can give it away. I've discovered that if I don't love myself—both in spirit, mind, and body—it is difficult to show others how I fully love them. Prior to meeting my husband, I had many boyfriends—some better than others. At times I felt like all I was doing was kissing frogs, and that I would never find my prince. The relationship I had prior to meeting my husband, Dan, was a huge eye opener. I was considered a young professional, making a nice salary, yet I was dating a very loving man, and not treating him with the respect that he deserved. He was an entrepreneur who was making a good living, but wasn't as organized and focused as I would have liked. As a result, I ended up hurting him and allowed myself to fall out of love with myself in the process. Looking back, there was a huge disconnect in our

5P's as a couple. Lucky for me, his parents were amazing people, and gave me a book, *Unconditional Love. Love without Limits*. My journey began and although we tried to make things work, we knew in our hearts that we were not meant to be life long partners.

A few months later, I met a good looking man who was worth millions at a Gettysburg College alumni winery event. I thought to myself, "Finally! The man I was searching for." We both quickly learned that we were not meant to be. I remember him asking me, "You are not the type of woman to stay home with the kids, are you?" After sharing with him some of my dreams, he gave me the greatest gift of all—my husband! They played soccer as kids and he was moving into his house in two weeks. Finally I was given a man who is good for me! It took my proclamation of my dreams and what I was looking for in a man, to be guided to my life partner. Although Dan was not *perfect*, he was perfect for me. I knew there was something special about him. Over time, he has turned out to be the best father and supporter I could have ever dreamed of having on my team!

Have we had up's and down's? Absolutely! When I started dating Dan, my mother warned me that he seemed to have many characteristic that reminded her of herself. At that point, I could have stopped dating him, but decided that I was going to be the judge! Although my entrepreneurial spirit that has developed over time certainly took him by surprise, we have worked hard to establish common ground and a common language for effective communication. In addition, we developed an awareness of our own personal 5P success strategies and attended a few professional development seminars together, including, Jack Canfield's

Business Success Principles workshop. Having said this, the application of the 5P's takes hard work. However, having this framework made it possible for us to love ourselves, enjoy our success, find peace, and raise our son in a loving, caring, nurturing family. I encourage you to share what you have learned in this book with those you love, complete the Star Power Actions, and come back together and share your answers. See how you can use it to strengthen your relationships, and both share and live your dreams.

Change "I Can't..." to "I Can..."

We've all said, "I can't do that because..." Life gives us plenty of opportunities to make excuses for why we can't do something.

> **Question:** What would have happened if I choose to hold onto these self-limiting beliefs to owning and operating a business? *"I can't open my own business because..."*

- I don't know how to set up a business.
- I don't have time.
- I can't while I'm still working full time.
- I'm terrible in math.
- I don't have the money.
- I don't know how to set up a website.
- I don't know how to use Photoshop.
- People won't buy my book.
- My network isn't big enough.
- My husband won't let me.
- I won't be there for my son.

Answer: I could have decided *not to* follow my dreams. That increases the likelihood of me being miserable at my job and home—which translates into low productivity, potential job loss, stress and health issues, marital problems, and a troubled child.

Now let's take it to the next level. When you say "I can't because..." you might as well be saying "I won't." Both words limit you from achieving your dreams. Write down something that you've always wanted to do, and list all the reasons why you haven't done it. Instead of using "I can't (insert dream) because..." I want you to substitute the word "won't" for "can't." Say both scenarios out loud. When you announce to the world you won't, it makes it more definitive. Scary, isn't it?

I mentioned earlier in this book that I use a strategy called positive reframing to get me through many of the negative thoughts that run through my mind. I also develop affirmations that help me visualize my success. Eliminate the reasons why you can't with affirmations and positive reframing! Make what seems impossible, possible. There are many reasons as to why you CAN achieve your dreams! Take your own obstacle, challenge, or dream, and apply these strategies to your own situation.

- **I don't know how to set up a business.**
  o SCORE (Service Corps of Retired Executives) can help me get started.
  o I have friends who own businesses who can help.
  o I can look on-line or buy a book for help on how to get started.
  o People who own businesses had to get started somewhere.

- **I don't have time.**
  - o What activities can I eliminate out of my daily routine (reduce amount of time I watch TV)?
  - o What activities do I need to delegate to friends and family next month (laundry, grocery shopping, and house cleaning)?
  - o How much vacation time from work am I willing to take to get started?
  - o What tasks do I need to accomplish? Approximately how long will each task take? What time do I have to dedicate this week?
  - o What schedule do I need to set up to have uninterrupted time?
  - o What behavioral changes do I need to make to give me more energy and keep me healthy (eat better, take natural energy boosters)?

- **I can't start a business while I'm still working full time.**
  - o See list above. I did it and so can you!
  - o It takes passion, persistence, and people, but it is possible!

- **I'm terrible in math.**
  - o Who cares! I can add, subtract, multiply and divide.

- **I don't have the money.**
  - o Where can I cut back and save in our current budget? What luxuries am I willing to give up?
  - o How much money do I really need to get started?
  - o What companies or people in my network might like to support what I am doing?

o What grant money is available?

o Who can I partner with?

o Develop a 12 slide business plan and identify cash flow vehicles.

- **I don't know how to set up a website.**

  o Who cares! I can set up a website at GoDaddy.com for less than $50.00. It's easy to do!

- **I don't know how to design marketing materials and logos.**

  o Who cares! There are 25 universities in the Philadelphia area who have students looking for design and marketing experience. It's a great way to keep things low cost!

- **People won't buy my book.**

  o Why wouldn't they? I have friends, who have friends, who have friends. It is called viral marketing... get the buzz going!

- **My network isn't big enough.**

  o How big is big? Just get out there and start attending free/low cost net working events.

  o Assess my current network. Build quality relationships. Eliminate those who are negative or those who bring you down.

- **My husband won't let me.**

  o Did I ask him? Did I share with him my fabulous vision and plan as to why it will work? Does he know what's in it for him?

- **I won't be there for my son.**
  o My son will gain more from me living my dream, than from me just doing the status-quo. What example do I want to set for him?

Turn I can't… I won't… into I can… and I will! Each day you need to work towards your goals. When developing goals, make sure they are SMART—specific, measureable, attainable, realistic and timely. You may not meet every single goal and you may fail miserably at times, but you have a better chance of being successful if you write them down. If you have negative thoughts and actions, focus on what you *don't* have, miss deadlines, make excuses and blame others, have low emotional intelligence or self-esteem, you have some work to do before setting out to live your dreams. Start by setting SMART goals around these challenges. Remember, it takes 21 days to make a new habit. Develop a chart like Ben Franklin did for his 13 virtues. Assess how you do each day. At the end of 21 days, look at how well you did and where you need to focus more of your energies. Once you conquer these obstacles, you will be more at peace and better equipped to achieve your long term goals and dreams.

Journal Your Way to Peace

There are three powerful journaling techniques I use when I'm feeling frustrated, angry, depressed, or sad. I can't tell you how many times people ask me, "Are you always this happy?" First of all, I have a few mantras I keep front of mind, such as, "every day is a holiday," "tomorrow is a grand new day," and "it could always be worse." Like most every person I know, I have ups and downs, and thankfully I've realized early in life that I have the power within myself to shift these feelings. One of the tools I use to regain focus is my irritations and tolerations list. There are three questions I ask myself and I journal about them for no more than 15 minutes. The three questions are:

- What is irritating me?
- How can I fix it?
- Who will I delegate all or part of fixing it to?

If what is irritating me is not in my control to fix, I have learned to let it go by reframing the situation. If I cannot fix something that is irritating me, I replace it with something that I can. If I continue to worry about it, I find my worry spot. My worry spot is in my walk in closet. It sounds bizarre, but it works. If I didn't have a spot that I dedicate solely to my worries, I would focus on things that hinder my happiness and progress whenever and wherever. My intentions would get clouded, and I would attract more of what I don't want in life.

Another journaling strategy I use is called a gratitude journal. You don't necessarily have to have a physical journal for any of these peace seeking strategies. Simply take out any piece of paper and in five minutes, write down as many things you can think of to be grateful for in your life. It can be a roof over your head, sunshine, loving family, your dog, you name it! It's your gratitude journal. If you get in the habit of doing this daily, it is a great way to set the tone for the rest of your day. The last journal I faithfully keep is only opened every three months. It is my appreciation list. Across the top of the sheet there are four questions: who do I appreciate, what do I appreciate about them, how can I express it, and when will I do it by. I give myself the next three months to express my gratitude. It not only makes them feel good, but it also gives me a feeling of peace and gratitude.

Choose to Live Mindfully

West Chester University's Stress Reduction Center brought Michael Carroll to campus last year with his important message of bringing mindfulness into the workplace. Carroll's book *The Mindful Leader* is an exceptional example of how we can be more productive if we live more in the here and now. You may be thinking it's an oxymoron, but it isn't. Being mindful doesn't mean you are not goals driven. It means you are living in the present moment and being present for others. You cultivate courage and confidence and lower anxiety and stress. Mindful living allows us to eliminate toxicity, appreciate health, build trust, send clear messages, embrace resistance, heal wounds and be realistic.

There was a time over the past three years that I was constantly looking into the future, not enjoying the present moment, and multi-tasking and thinking all of the time. As a result, my stress level rose and my relationship with my husband began to suffer. Others who fail to live mindfully might also experience forgetfulness, miss deadlines, or feel they can't do anything well.

When I heard Michael speak, it brought awareness to where I needed to make a change. In the back of my mind I thought that if I begin to live more mindfully, I will begin to miss opportunities and it will take me off my goals. I did not want to lose my husband, so I began to train myself on how to live more mindfully. I discovered that I could become calmer, deeper, more centered person. Everyone wins!

Below is my list of 15 mindful living commitments. I haven't been able to master all of them yet, but just as Ben Franklin did with his virtues, I keep track. Some weeks are definitely better than others, but I am beginning with the end in mind. I encourage you to assess how you are currently committing to living mindfully, and where you would like to see improvement. What steps are you willing to take to live more mindfully?

1. **Do one thing at a time.** Single-task, don't multi-task. When you're pouring water, just pour water. When you're eating, just eat. When you're bathing, just bathe. Don't try to knock off a few tasks while eating or bathing or driving. Also, according to Steven Covey, if you are taken off task, it takes you 15 minutes to get you back on task once you are taken off. Think about how much time you could waste in a given day. See what you can do to limit interruptions.

2. **Do less.** Figure out what's important, and let go of what's not. Stop the busy-work. Instead of running around doing lots of little things—slow down and manage the tasks. Group them appropriately. Categorize them on a priority scale. I use Steve Covey's Time Matrix to plan my four quadrants—what to do immediately, what tasks are proactive, what needs delegated, and what needs eliminated. It allows you to spend more time in the quadrant of productivity. Live a calmer, more peaceful life.

3. **Put space between things.** Manage your schedule so that you always have time to complete each task. Don't schedule things close together — instead, leave room between things on your schedule. That gives you a more relaxed schedule, and leaves space in case one task takes longer than you planned. Also, figure how much time is

spent being interrupted. See how you can minimize it and plan your tasks accordingly.

4. Spend at least 5 minutes each day doing nothing. Just sit in silence. Become aware of your thoughts. Focus on your breathing. Notice the world around you. Become comfortable with the silence and stillness. I still have not been able to master this one in its entirety, but this is when you can try to practice it:

- During a coffee break
- While stopped at a traffic light or stop sign
- While waiting in line at the bank or grocery store
- When put on hold on the telephone, while hearing that message about how important your call is
- While the computer is booting up or loading a program
- Between meetings or phone calls.

5. Stop worrying about the future - focus on the present. Spend more time in the moment. We worry too much, and it does us no good. We think about things that haven't happened, instead of what's happening now. And while some planning is necessary, too much of it is a waste of time — there's no way to predict the future, and trying to control every little thing that's going to happen is futile. Learn to go with the flow, look for opportunities, find the natural path of things, and do what is needed in the moment. You can't control outcomes, but if you learn to work more fluidly, you can get to amazing outcomes.

6. When you're talking to someone, be present. How many of us have spent time with someone, but have been thinking about what we need to do in the future? Or thinking about what we want to say next, instead of really listening to that person? Instead, focus on being present, on really listening, on really enjoying your time with that person.

7. **Eat slowly and savor your food.** Food can be crammed down our throats in a rush, but where's the joy in that? Savor each bite, slowly, and really get the most out of your food. Interestingly, you'll eat less this way, and digest your food better as well.

8. **Live slowly and savor your life.** Just as you would savor your food by eating it more slowly, do everything this way — slow down and savor each and every moment. When you are spending time with your children, focus just on them.

9. **Make cleaning and cooking become meditation.** Cooking and cleaning are often seen as drudgery, but actually they are both great ways to practice mindfulness, and can be great rituals performed each day. If cooking and cleaning seem like boring chores to you, try doing them as a form of meditation. Put your entire mind into those tasks, concentrate, and do them slowly and completely. It could change your entire day (as well as leave you with a cleaner house).

10. **Go the speed limit and enjoy the drive.** I use less gas, get less frustrated, and have less of a chance of getting into an accident. A win-win for everyone!

11. **Automate systems.** Your finances, your house, your phone, computer tasks, shopping...everything! The less you need to think about and remember, the better off you will be.

12. **Buy less.** If you spend less, shop less, and acquire less, you will own less, need less, get into less debt, be in better financial shape, have less clutter, and have more time for things that are truly important.

13. **Limit excessive communication.** When you do communicate, make it count, make it sincere, and more than you talk, listen. Make every email count. Only IM when it's necessary. Spend less time on the phone, Twitter your Blackberry or iPhone, and more time with humans, more time with yourself, and more time in the present.

14. **Eliminate complaining and criticizing.** I won't rant about how these two things can drag down you and those around you ... but instead, I will say that if you did less of these two things, your life would be better. We all do them to some extent. Fess up! Instead, do more kindness, compassion, understanding, accepting, and loving.

15. **Judge less.** Acceptance is something I'm trying to learn to do more. And that means I need to be less judgmental, and stop having expectations from everything and everybody. Accepting people for who they are leads to peace and happiness. People won't disappoint you because you'll learn to accept them as they are, and learn that they are already perfect, as they are.

Make time for you

Have you ever heard the story where if you are ever in a plane accident, put the mask on you first, then your children? The number one complaint of people in general is that they don't have enough time. This means that we're too busy putting on an oxygen mask on everyone else but ourselves. Even when we do have a moment to ourselves, the feeling of self imposed guilt sometimes creeps in to tell us we should be doing something. If you are one of the smart ones, you already have scheduled your "me" time in advance to make sure you get it. For those who don't schedule it, it's not too late. "Me" time sometimes translates into an evening out, but it doesn't have to. Also, who says that it has to be a full evening? You might be satisfied with a 30 minute break each day or even every other day.

That's why I am going to encourage you to list things that you can do to find peace depending on the situation. Here is my list:

15 minutes
o Stretch/yoga
o Quiet time/breathe
o Write in my journal
o Listen to music
o Enjoy a glass of wine
o Check personal e-mail/social media
o Drink tea by myself
o Call a friend/family member

1 hour
o Read a book/magazine
o Relaxing bath
o Visit the local library or coffee shop
o Manicure/massage
o Lounge on a hammock
o Put together a puzzle
o Write more books and inspirational music

2 hours
o Go for a hike/walk
o Go to the pool
o Go for a drive
o Visit a museum
o Take an art class

3 hours

- o Go to a happy hour
- o Go to a movie
- o Go to a friend's house
- o Go to a charity event
- o Go kayaking
- o Watch a play at a local theatre

STAR POWER ACTIONS

1.) What are some self-limiting beliefs you have been told over the years either by others or yourself? How have you planned for or what is your plan to overcome these irrational beliefs?

2.) What do you love about yourself? What would others say they admire about you? How can you strengthen these qualities?

3.) What are some things you would change about yourself or your current situation in life? Do you believe you can change them, and if so, how do you plan to change them and by when?

4.) What or who is stopping you from achieving your goals? How are you going to minimize their power over you?

5.) Who in your life do you appreciate? What do you appreciate about them and how could you express it? When will you do it by?

6.) For the next 15 minutes, write down the things you are grateful for in life.

7.) How are you going to choose to live mindfully? If you need help, look at my list of 15 commitments.

8.) List the things that you will do when you make time for yourself—15 minutes, 1 hour, 2 hours, and 3 hours.

**"Don't compromise yourself.
You are all you've got."**

*–Janis Joplin, American singer,
songwriter and music arranger*

CLOSING THOUGHTS FROM MOLLY SUNSHINE

Now that you have read my story to *Chasing Stars in the Sunshine*, it's time for you to "peel the sunshine." Yep, forget the onion! You have to get to your core and start taking star powered actions. It's your choice whether you use the free companion guide or start by tackling one *Star Power Action* found at the end of each chapter. Inaction is not an option! We have been given too short of a time here on earth for you to spend it wallowing in what you don't have or becoming an energy zapper for someone else. It's not always easy; however, what is easy is making the time to plan for your own success. Start taking one or two small steps towards living your dreams each day… *starting today!*

There are opportunities that are out there just waiting for you to uncover. Whatever the opportunity, don't expect them to magically appear. Increase your chances of achieving your dreams—align your 5 P's and live your legacy to the Nth degree. Identify your **Principles**, and match your words, thoughts and actions with your core **Passions**, and you will attract the **People** and **Persistence** you need to shoot for the stars. You will be rewarded with a new sense of **Peace**.

No matter what the outcome, there is one guarantee; no action leads outcomes determined by others. What are you waiting for? Your legacy awaits you! Get out there and *Chase Stars in the Sunshine* and activate your *5 P's to Achieving Your Dreams*! My life's mission is to *"make a difference and be the difference!"* If you need help reaching your goals, add me to your oikos. Send me an e-mail at molly@legacyproducers.com. I'll do everything in my Molly Sunshine power to help you achieve your dreams.

Shine on!

Molly

ACKNOWLEDGEMENTS

There are many people who make it possible for me to live my legacy. My love and gratitude go out to my husband, Dan, and son, Tyler, who constantly support me with their gifts of love and compassion, and give me the time to create and inspire others to make a difference.

To my mother and father for giving me your love, guidance, work ethic, values, and opportunities to learn and experience the world. We may not have always seen eye to eye, but you have always given me the room to grow and discover. Thank you!

To Scott Sherman, my supervisor at West Chester University, for encouraging my growth as I rapidly expanded my skills and adventures and put my 5 P's into overdrive.

To Anthony Gold who inspired me to take my first leap into the world of entrepreneurism.

To Michael Pearson who graciously helped me realize my first company, MyInternshipGopher.com, with his technical expertise and patience.

To Dave Magrogan, for believing in me and giving me the creative freedom to build the Rhino Living brand and co-author our first book. Thank you for modeling the way and supporting me in my own Molly Sunshine motivational speaking adventures. Here's to Rhinos and Sunshine!

To Dan Murphy for being my #1 editor and can-do man with anything techie.

To all my Sunshine women. You know who you are! Keep making a difference, and being the difference. Thank you for your amazing support. The 2010 Molly Sunshine Tour is dedicated to you!

Lastly and most importantly, thank you God for giving me the strength and determination to lift people up to their fullest potential and face a negative world with a smile and a limitless list of possibilities.

ABOUT THE AUTHOR

Molly Nece attributes much of her success to her positive mental outlook, her assertiveness, and her ability to strengthen and align her 5 P's to realizing her dreams. Through her coaching, consulting and production company, Legacy Producers, she's been able to help people discover their legacy, find fulfillment in life and share their legacy with others to the Nth degree! Molly also serves as President of Rhino Living Training Group and CEO of MyInternshipGopher.com. If that wasn't enough, she is also West Chester University's Senior Internal Consultant and founder of the Molly Sunshine Tour.

Molly is known for always going the extra mile no matter what project she takes on. She also looks for a fit within her personal mission—to make a difference and be the difference. Her Molly Sunshine Tour, Miss Molly Sunshine children's book series, and business adventures are all great examples of her dedication to living her legacy and fulfilling that mission.

Early in life, Molly discovered her passion was guiding people to find their full potential and giving them the skills they need to be successful in life. Although she graduated with an elementary education degree, her career in higher education varied from a small private liberal arts women's college in Pittsburgh, a highly selective private liberal arts college in Gettysburg to a large state university in West Chester, Pennsylvania. After spending most of her career in higher education, Wells Fargo Educational Financial Services recruited her into sales and marketing. Although a sales and marketing superstar, she felt unfulfilled.

After saying goodbye to the corporate world, she completed her Masters in Training and Organizational Development at West Chester University and received her Lean Six Sigma Certificate from Villanova University. Shortly after, she was asked to join West Chester University's Office of Training and Organizational Development. Over the past 10 years, she's been able to design and deliver hundreds of professional development training programs, and has inspired tens of thousands of students, faculty, staff, and external organizations, and coached and consulted hundreds of business leaders and their front lines. Molly is committed to modeling the way through her 5 P's—*Principles, Passions, People, Persistence, and Peace*, and enjoys inspiring others to put into action the 5 P's to living their dreams.